I0606588

If these canisters of biological weapons had fallen into terrorists' hands, it could be catastrophic…

When the lawyer arrived, Steiner and Shavbiz took the interview chairs opposite Perrez and his lawyer, Yashina.

"If your client doesn't fully cooperate, Mr. Yashina, then the State of Israel will assume that he's actively involved in biological terrorism," Steiner said.

Yashina surprised Steiner by smiling. "Let me be clear, Inspector," he said. "My client ordered Russian tractor parts. However, it appears that criminals may have used this container to smuggle biological weapons into Israel. My client is a man with an unblemished character, and is now under threat of incarceration solely because he was an easy target for smugglers."

Steiner had already taken a dislike to Yashina, whom he saw as a typical smug lawyer with an attitude. Yashina was the type of man who made a policeman's life impossible. Steiner could see that they had a long session ahead of them.

If the canisters had been smuggled into Israel, using Perrez's container, then time was against them. Every second wasted could be a second closer to some fanatic using them. It then left—

Steiner didn't want to contemplate what it left.

Sarah Appleton has been kidnapped from her university campus in Cambridge, England. When she escapes, killing her abductor, she sets in motion a chain of events that has repercussions all across the world. Sarah and her father, Martin Appleton, flee the Russian mafia, from whom Martin stole twenty million dollars in bearer bonds, leaving authorities to unravel the threat of a terrorist plot using biological weapons of mass destruction stolen from a Russian lab and sold to Middle Eastern extremists. As the authorities scramble to unravel the scant clues left by people who make few mistakes, terrorists gear up for an attack that will leave millions of innocent people dead and the governments of several Middle Eastern nations in chaos.

KUDOS for *Disciples of Death*

In *Disciples of Death* by Paul Howard, Sarah Appleton is kidnapped because her father stole twenty million dollars from the Russian mafia. After Sarah escapes, she and her father flee under assumed names, with the mafia close on their heels. As the authorities investigate, they are left with a bunch of unanswered questions, such as what the mafia has done with a load of biological weapons they stole from a Russian lab. Now it is a race against time to track down the weapons before terrorists can attack and cause millions of innocent deaths. The story is very fast paced and filled with surprises, both for the characters and the readers. It will grab your interest at the beginning and hang onto it right through the end. *~ Taylor Jones, Reviewer*

Disciples of Death by Paul Howard is the story of a group of Middle Eastern terrorists who plan an attack on other Middle Eastern countries, using biological weapons of mass destruction. The book takes us through the maneuverings of the Russian mafia, the subterfuge of the terrorist cell, and the desperate plight of a man and his daughter after the man stole $20,000,000 in bearer bonds from the Russian mafia. When the authorities get involved—after a mafia assassin finds the man and his daughter—the investigation goes international and the hunt for stolen biological weapons the mafia sold to some terrorists begins. *Disciples of Death* is a cleverly told story, in the manner of Tom Clancy, with a strong plot that's full of twists and turns. Its fast -paced, tension-filled action will have you turning pages well into the night. *~ Regan Murphy, Reviewer*

Disciples of Death

Paul Howard

A Black Opal Books Publication

GENRE: THRILLER/SUSPENSE

This is a work of fiction. Names, places, characters and incidents are either the product of the author's imagination or are used fictitiously, and any resemblance to any actual persons, living or dead, businesses, organizations, events or locales is entirely coincidental. All trademarks, service marks, registered trademarks, and registered service marks are the property of their respective owners and are used herein for identification purposes only. The publisher does not have any control over or assume any responsibility for author or third-party websites or their contents.

DEDICATION

*Special thanks to Jack Phillips for helping me
to get here and to Faye for her patience.
Anna-Maria, my love always.
Regrets, only one—my deceased parents,
Mike and Hilda, aren't here to read the book.*

Chapter 1

Death was easy to find if you looked for it. Artie Grimshaw had found it on many occasions in his life. He wouldn't kill the girl just yet. There were things he needed to know about her father first. She'd make a good bargaining tool. Girls always did. Fathers always had a soft spot for their daughters. He presumed Appleton was a good father. He was a shit in most things in life, but surely this fit young thing would nurture the fatherly instincts, even in him.

Murder didn't bother Grimshaw. Murder had always been a constant bedfellow in his life. He looked at the terrified girl, lying bound and gagged on the bed, and wondered if she realized this was almost her moment to die? The victim never did, up until the end—they always believed there was hope.

Grimshaw stared out the grimy caravan window at the rain lashing in off the North Sea. How could a place be such a wonderful holiday haven in the summer and yet so bleak and depressing in winter? Grimshaw needed to bring Appleton to him, find out what the bastard had done with the stolen money.

Grimshaw watched the girl's smooth shaven legs wriggling in her bonds and felt a perverted sexual attraction. Tasty bait. Was it bait enough to bring Appleton to him? He'd make the girl give him Appleton's mobile number shortly. Maybe he'd have some fun first, show the girl that older men could be just as sexually demanding as the young ones.

"Fucking weather!" he grumbled.

He swigged some of his beer and then walked into the cramped toilet. Caravans were always so fucking cramped, the decaying world of sad, gray pensioners. He remembered awful memories of childhood when his drippy parents had caught the camping bug and, every holiday, had dragged him around the campsites of England. He shut the door behind him. The girl was secure, the caravan door locked. Even Grimshaw needed privacy for some moments in his life.

After the toilet door shut, the girl frantically struggled with her bonds. She could feel the left hand loosening. Twisting, writhing her body, somehow she found the strength to move her numb hands. The ropes had dug deeply, her blood circulation had been squeezed, so she could barely move her hands. If she could free just one of them…

Her senses were alive with fear and tension. Every creak and sound from the toilet was amplified in her head.

If she could just free a hand. One hand would give her hope. She could feel the rope slackening. In the toilet, the monster was singing some dreadful Chas and Dave song she remembered hearing an uncle play years ago. The knot finally wriggled loose, her hand was free.

Numb hands didn't make for easy work. The blood was slowly pulsating through her veins. The circulation was coming back, as she frantically removed the rest of her bonds. The sound of violently flushing water—the chain had been pulled, the monster was almost upon her.

A matter of seconds. She stared at the gun on the table that had held her eyes in morbid fascination since her kidnapping. She reached, grabbed. Her shaking hands somehow managed to cling to it just as the monster arrived back in the room.

She removed the safety catch. All that reading of detective fiction in her formative years at last came in useful.

When Grimshaw entered the room and saw the gun pointing at him, his eyes were suddenly alert and attentive. The High Power Browning was shaking in the terrified girl's hand. "Take it easy, darling, you could have a serious accident with that."

"Don't move!" the girl shouted.

Grimshaw nervously edged a step forward.

"Don't move!"

Grimshaw smiled confidently. "I work with killers every day, see what it takes to become one. I can take one look in your eyes and see that they're not the eyes of a killer." Grimshaw stopped and paused. "I know you won't use it, darling. You probably don't know how to."

Grimshaw walked toward the gun. The girl fired twice into his torso. The bullets ripped into his heart ventricles. Grimshaw stared blankly, unable to comprehend his misjudgement. He fell and died on the floor. Blood seeped across the faded linoleum. The girl rushed to the toilet and was violently sick in the basin. She retched and remained there for several minutes. After rinsing her mouth and wiping it, she returned to the living room.

The room was silent when she returned, the sound of rain lashing against the window the only accompaniment to the bleak Orwellian scene. In a table drawer, she found her confiscated mobile phone. She frantically checked it, grateful it still had enough charge. She dialled her father. She'd killed a man. She'd killed a man, but he'd kidnapped her. Surely, killing in self-defence couldn't count as murder.

Her father answered on the third ring.

"Dad, I'm in trouble!" she shouted.

"You're not pregnant—"

"Of course I'm not pregnant. You have to listen to me. I've killed a man."

"Killed a man—"

"He kidnapped me, gave me no choice," she tried to explain. "He kidnapped me off of campus—it was horrible—"

"Keep calm, Sarah! If you stay calm, we can get you through this."

"I need to call the police."

"Don't call the police, darling. You killed a man. We have to think about what we're doing."

"Think about? What's there to think about?"

"Where are you?" Appleton asked nervously.

"I don't know. The sign outside the caravan says Caister. It's a caravan park."

"Caister's in Norfolk," Appleton said. "I'll be there in two hours. When I get there, I'll ring you for further directions."

Appleton hung up. Sarah stared blankly at the dead body. She'd killed a man. She'd killed a man, and she wasn't sure if there were any other kidnappers around. She grabbed the gun, clutched it as if her life depended on it. Dad should've told her to call the police. Why hadn't he told her to call the police?

The thought kept regurgitating through her head.

She stood by the window and stared at some nearby bushes being buffeted by the wind. There was no sign of a car. She'd been brought here in a car. She tried to focus, remember. An intruder had chloroformed her as she opened her car door.

Everything after that was blank until she'd woken, bound, on the bed.

She went outside to find out where she was. At the corner of the road, she found a sign with the campsite name. When her father rang, she had a brief directional conversation with him, and, shortly after, she could see darting headlights coming along the coast road toward her.

It was her father. His trademark erratic driving took him to the other side of the campsite. Sarah rushed out on the grass and waved him toward her. The Rover slid to a halt in the clawing mud close to the caravan. Appleton stepped out of the car, held his daughter a moment in a reassuring hug.

"It's going to be okay, just stay calm, darling." He patted his daughter on the back, attempting to reassure her. The shell-shocked look on her pale face told him she would take some reassuring.

A squally downpour battered them so they scurried inside. Appleton took in the grisly scene of Grimshaw lying in a pool of blood. Sarah shook Appleton from his reverie by bursting into tears. "I think he was going to kill me."

Appleton held his daughter as she cried. "It's okay, Sarah, I'm here now. We'll sort this mess out." Appleton gently brushed her hair with his hand. "I want you to go over everything that happened, give me some details."

"It all happened so quickly. I went to my car. He jumped me. He thrust a chloroformed cloth over my mouth. I thought he was trying to smother me. I fought for breath—blacked out. When I awoke, I found myself tied up on the bed."

Appleton looked at Grimshaw's body. Grimshaw was a twisted motherfucker who had a catalogue of violent assaults and a couple of rapes on his rap sheet. Appleton's head was filled with horror at the thought of Sarah at his mercy. He must've been acting independently. If he'd been acting with Winterburn's blessing, then Winterburn would be here torturing information out of Sarah. "We'd better get rid of the body."

Sarah angrily pulled away from her father. "Get rid of it? Why would we need to get rid of the body? We need to ring the police. I was kidnapped. Shooting him will just go down as self-defence."

Appleton sighed. "We can't ring the police, love."

"The police have to be told! Nobody is going to blame me for killing him, under the circumstances.

"You can't ring the police, love."

Sarah glared at her father. "We need to ring the police. He might not have been working alone."

Appleton walked to the window and stared into the night. "He was working alone."

Sarah stormed over to her father and jerked him around so he was looking at her. "How do you know he was working alone?"

"Trust me on this, Sarah. He was working alone. He was working alone, trying to get an angle on his boss to use for financial gain." Appleton paused. "These people work outside the law, and there are reasons why we can't go to the police."

"That man kidnapped me at gunpoint. In my escape, I shot him to survive. No court is ever going to look at me in anything other than a sympathetic light."

"If you go to the police, we're as good as dead."

Sarah stared blankly at Appleton. She was starting to realize how little she knew him. "What have you been doing, Dad?"

"It's complicated."

"Isn't it always?" she snapped.

"There are some people I work for. It's not a case of

what I've been doing. It's more a case of what I haven't been doing."

She grabbed him. "It's one of your fucking deals. I nearly got killed because of one of your fucking deals."

She pulled away and started toward the door.

"Where are you going?" Appleton asked.

"I need some air." She opened the door and stood there, looking out into the chilly rain-washed night.

Appleton slowly walked up to his daughter, leaned on her cold bare shoulders. "You can't go anywhere now that you've killed Grimshaw. Artie has some powerful friends. He must've told someone he had you. They'll find out you've killed him, and they'll come after us."

"And how would you know that?"

"I do the accounts for his boss, Winterburn. Grimshaw works for one of the London firms—"

"You told me you were out of all that shit!" Sarah rounded on him. "After Mum died, you promised me you'd get out of all that and go into legitimate business."

"I'm sorry, Sarah, you don't get out that easy."

"Anyone can get out if they want to!" She shook her head. "You've never wanted to. You've always pretended you're something you're not, you think you're big time when you're just a plastic gangster."

"And that's what you think of me?"

"It's what I know, Dad."

Appleton went out to his car and returned with his briefcase. He put the briefcase on a table and clicked it open. From inside, he took out some bearer bonds and laid them on the table. "If I'm just small time, then what do you make of these?"

Sarah's delicate fingers ran through the bearer bonds, the sapphire blue of her eyes more predominant in the darkness. "You stole these from the person this Grimshaw worked for."

"Grimshaw was just a lackey. Now, Josh Winter-burn, who Grimshaw worked for, Winterburn is the real deal."

"You stole these from this Winterburn?"

"Yes, darling."

"How could you? You're messing with psychos. I'm your daughter." She stared at Appleton, uncomprehend-ing. "If you put your life in danger, you put mine in danger, too."

"Don't panic, love. I've got enough money here for us to make a new life together somewhere."

"I don't want a new life," she protested, "I'm happy with my old one."

"I'm sorry, love."

He was always sorry, Sarah thought. Dad was always sorry, and other people had to clean up the mess. She didn't know much about her life now. One thing she did know—from this moment on, she was on the run and it could last indefinitely.

Chapter 2

You don't seem to understand how precarious your position is, Rob," Winterburn said, sitting on the edge of an old desk.

He rubbed the blade of a Stanley knife on the desk, cutting off some fragments of wood. In the background, Alan Fordsham, Winterburn's trusty lieutenant, stood menacingly in the shadows of the poorly lit room.

"Please, Mr. Winterburn," Rob Barnet pleaded, terrified, with sweat oozing from every pore of his body. "I don't know anything."

"I dread to think what your face will look like when Alan's finished with you." Winterburn paused for effect. Looking at the fear in Barnet's eyes, it was obvious he was contemplating his impending disfigurement. "When Alan's finished with you, the elephant man would look like a Paris fashion model compared to you, Rob."

"Appleton didn't tell me anything—I've barely spoken to him in recent weeks." Barnet was unable to look Winterburn in the eye.

Winterburn grabbed Barnet's face and tried to force Barnet to engage his stare. Barnet averted Winterburn's gaze. Winterburn slapped Barnet across the face and stepped backward.

A stunned Barnet at last looked at him.

"Two days ago you were seen with Appleton in a pub in Stepney," Winterburn paused. "You're not making this easy for me, Rob. I keep looking at you as just guilty by association. If you keep lying to me, I'm going to start assuming you know much more than I think you do."

Fordsham walked over behind Barnet. Winterburn handed Fordsham the Stanley knife. Fordsham studied the sharp blade and smiled. "I'll get him to talk in under ten minutes, Mr. Winterburn," he promised. He slashed the Stanley knife a few times in the air like Zorro to emphasize the point.

"I bumped into him in the pub, Mr. Winterburn," Barnet quickly offered, his terrified eyes watching Fordsham's every movement. "I barely spoke to him—just passed the time of day."

"It's now or never, Rob. If you know anything, I strongly urge you to tell me while you've still got a face left." Winterburn stepped back and Fordsham stepped forward in Barnet's eye line. "I'm not going to be able to keep Alan on a leash for much longer, Rob. You have to ask yourself if Appleton is worth all this aggro?"

Barnet looked uneasily at Fordsham and quickly came to a decision. "Okay, Mr. Winterburn, I'll tell you everything I know. Just keep that psycho away from me," he said hurriedly.

Winterburn gave Fordsham the nod. Fordsham stepped back a pace and put the Stanley knife down.

"Appleton contacted me a few weeks ago. He asked me to make him a passport and driving licence, said he needed them in case of emergency. I thought he was working for you, Mr. Winterburn. If I'd known he wasn't, I'd never have made it for him." Barnet looked at Winterburn pleadingly. "I didn't know he'd gone independent, honestly, Mr. Winterburn."

"Okay, Rob, let's just say you were given a bum steer. I'll release your hands, and I want you to write down the details of everything you gave him." Winterburn brushed his hand reassuringly on Barnet's sweaty cheek. "No mistakes, Rob. I can't emphasize how important it is to me that you give me everything."

Barnet's handcuffs were unlocked, and he rubbed his stiff hands to get the circulation moving. Winterburn took a notepad and pen from the foreman's drawer and handed it to Barnet. Barnet grabbed the pen and started to write. He wrote frantically like a dead man who'd been given a lifeline. He took off his coat then ripped open the lining. From the lining of his coat, Barnet took out a slip of paper with forged numbers written on it.

"Very clever, Rob." Winterburn admired the creep's nerve, sitting there with all that info in the lining of his jacket while being interrogated.

Barnet pointed at a number on the sheet. "That's the passport number, Mr. Winterburn. The passport is under that name. If he's on the run, that's the name Appleton will be using as an alias."

Winterburn looked at the number and smiled the smile of a man in complete control. Barnet was like an eager-to-please puppy. "I hope so, Rob. A lot, including your future wellbeing, depends on this."

Winterburn stepped behind Barnet, playfully ruffling Barnet's hair. "You've done very well, Rob, I'm very pleased with you."

Winterburn slipped a silenced Beretta from his jacket pocket. This was the moment that he enjoyed the most. Killing a man could be a pleasure if approached in the right way. Seeing the look of relief in the victim's eyes, that hopeful expression. They'd given you what you want so why would you kill them? All that hope and grabbing for life obliterated so quickly.

Winterburn fired the Beretta twice into the back of Barnet's head. Barnet's head flopped forward, blood and bone splattering the floor. When the body settled in the chair, Winterburn turned to Fordsham. "Get rid of him."

Fordsham picked up Barnet's chubby body, carried it outside, and dumped it in the Daimler's boot. The lights of the city glimmered off the shimmering Thames. Sewage stench drifted off the river, wafting into Fordsham's nostrils.

He locked the boot and stepped back inside. "Are you coming with me, Mr. Winterburn?"

"No, I need to stay here and make some calls."

Fordsham left. Winterburn glanced at Appleton's new passport name. Brian Hopper.

Winterburn knew Barnet was telling the truth. Instinct told him so. In Winterburn's world, you lived by instinct. Instinct had kept him at the top for all these years. Instinct meant the difference between life and death in the dark underworld he inhabited.

From a musty smelling cleaner's cupboard Winterburn got a mop and bucket and cleaned the blood-splattered floor. He was always thorough. Forensic science was moving on in leaps and bounds. Only the stupid criminal wasn't aware of it and failed to take note of the advances. Satisfied, he picked up the phone on the foreman's desk. Winterburn owned the company, another dodgy subsidiary. He dialled long distance.

A Russian woman answered.

"I'd like to speak to Kranjenkov," Winterburn asked in his stuttering Russian.

"Kranjenkov isn't here at the moment," the woman offered.

Winterburn noted the caution in her voice. The fucking Russians didn't like to commit. They were wary after all those years under the Communists.

"Would you give him a message, please? Tell him his English friend called. Tell him I'll call again the same time tomorrow."

"I'll tell him." She hung up.

Brief and to the point. Hardly the eloquence of Chekov, more the abruptness of a Boris Yeltsin.

Winterburn wondered if Kranjenkov would ever get the message? He'd met Kranjenkov once. He'd flown to Moscow when they were making the deal. Winterburn liked to do his deals face-to-face, look his adversary in the eye. They'd rendezvoused in the sleazy lap dancing bar that Winterburn had just rung. The deal of a lifetime. It had been the deal to ensure Winterburn's retirement to his villa in the South of France.

How had Appleton managed to steal twenty million from him? Winterburn wasn't a patsy, not a new kid on the block. The twenty million had been the first of five instalments culminating in a hundred million. The payment of a hundred million was for Winterburn signing over control of his various assets to the Russians.

How had he underestimated Appleton so badly? Appleton knew what Winterburn would do to him if he crossed him, and still he'd done it. For a man like Winterburn, used to ruling his underworld empire with fear and intimidation, it was hard to understand. How did Appleton suddenly have the balls to do this to him?

Appleton's theft meant Winterburn hadn't received the first Russian instalment. The bearer bonds had been delivered by the Moscow courier. They were supposed to be in a safety deposit box in a Central London bank. Appleton was meant to have seen to it.

When Winterburn suddenly couldn't get hold of Appleton, he became suspicious. A hurried visit to the bank by a flustered Winterburn proved that the safety deposit box was empty.

Winterburn furiously smashed his fist against the wall, dislodging worn plaster. A ring of blood appeared around his knuckles. He grabbed a hanky from the drawer and wiped the blood off his fingers. He decided he needed to get a punching bag installed for such moments when his dark rages got the better of him. He left the office and went to his Mercedes. On his mobile, he called Taylor and arranged a meeting. Appleton didn't know Winterburn knew his alias, so there was still a chance.

A red-faced Taylor in a flower-patterned dressing gown greeted Winterburn on the marble steps of his lavish Holland Park home. As Winterburn entered, a blond-haired rent boy left. Winterburn eyed the boy aggressively, his expression unable to mask his disgust. "I'm sorry, Mr. Winterburn, I'd arranged for Aaron to come over before you rang."

Winterburn didn't comment, but just elbowed past Taylor into the perfume smelling living room. Winterburn coughed. "This place smells like a fucking boudoir, Taylor."

Taylor joined him. "Like I said, I wasn't expecting you, Mr. Winterburn. I was about to entertain, I'd have cancelled if you'd called me earlier."

Winterburn sat on a red leather sofa, noting the chintzy direction of the room's décor. It looked like a poof's room, it was a poof's room. "It doesn't matter. I've got bigger things on the agenda than your perversity, Taylor."

Taylor's face reddened.

"I'm looking for someone using an alias. That someone is going to attempt to leave the country. They might have already left. That's up to you to find out for me."

"You want a hunt and search?" Taylor asked.

"Quickly. Top priority. You drop all other work for this."

"It'll cost ten grand."

"It's usually five—"

"I've got several jobs on the go at the moment," Taylor quickly defended. "The urgency in your voice tells me you want this done immediately. It means I'll have to farm out the other work to some of my associates—"

"I don't need a bloody lecture, just do what you have to." Winterburn took out two bundles of notes from his pocket and threw them on the table. "A word of warning—for this kind of fee, I expect you to find him."

"I can only guarantee success if you've got something to aid my search, Mr. Winterburn."

Winterburn handed Taylor a piece of paper with Appleton's alias details on. "That's the name he'll be using. He'll have a British passport and credit cards in that name."

"Okay, we'll go to my study."

Winterburn followed Taylor into his book-lined study.

"I need silence while I work."

"You're the only one talking," Winterburn growled.

He sat on a comfortable sofa. Taylor's place reeked of money. It showed that business was good for the gay twat.

Taylor set to work on his computer. He'd start with the airlines. If the subject had flown, there'd be something. "This could take hours, Mr. Winterburn." He quickly decided to emphasize that it would take time. He had heard of Winterburn's dark rages when things didn't go as planned.

"I'll wait. This is the most important thing in my life."

Winterburn wouldn't leave. Appleton was everything. Appleton was all he'd see at night in his dreams until the fucker was found. Appleton had pulled the big grift on Winterburn, and Winterburn wasn't going to let him get away with it.

All he could see was Appleton, somewhere warm and sunny, laughing at him. It wasn't just about the money. Although the money was his main focus, he also had other concerns. Appleton's actions had cost Winterburn respect, made him look foolish in front of the Russians. It showed Winterburn one thing—it showed him he was getting too old for this game. It was time to get out, but first, revenge, retribution, retrieving the money—all these things would have to be achieved before he could retire in peace.

The Russians could be brutal. Winterburn had heard reports of their violence from associates. They'd now paid the first instalment. In their eyes, Winterburn was now theirs. Twenty bloody million. Winterburn wanted to stand over Taylor with a Beretta squeezing into Taylor's head to get him moving.

Winterburn would stand back. In this business, you had to know when to be patient and when to shove. He wanted to shove, hard, push things along. Alas, that wasn't possible. These things took time, an infinitesimal amount of time—time, Winterburn decided, he might not have.

Chapter 3

What a fucking dive," Sergeant Miloslav Rominev of the Moscow Police said, studying the flickering neon lights of the nightclub across the road in the sleety rain.

"All such places are dives, Sergeant," Captain Alexi Pradischi said. Pradischi had long ago decided on that fact. The clubs were sleazy and so were all the people who frequented them.

There were two drunks arguing with a burly doorman, a typical night at the Glasnost a Go Go. Pradischi sighed, opened the glove compartment of his car, and took out a packet of fags. He lit one and dragged on it, amused at the discomfort in Rominev's eyes as the smoke wafted over the non-smoking sergeant's face.

"Why are we here, sir?" Rominev asked.

"Nikolai Kranjenkov, the owner of the club, is a broker for the Russian mafia. Kranjenkov's associates are responsible for half the crack abuse in the city. They're also responsible for the illicit foreign arms trade. You name it, he's into it. He's a very dangerous man, Sergeant, reason enough to keep an eye on him."

"If he's into all these things and dangerous, then why haven't we taken the bastard out, sir?"

"Although we know that Kranjenkov is a mafia broker, he's untouchable. We need to know what they're doing. Through Kranjenkov, we have a window into their world. The moment we arrest him, they know we're onto them and we drive them underground."

"Why are we waiting here this time of the night, sir?"

"We're here because I'm waiting for one of the dancers to finish. Mischa, a dancer at the club, is an undercover policewoman. She was transferred from Perm for this operation. We couldn't afford to risk a local, someone who might be known to them."

"Probably wise, sir. The fuckers always seem to know the local cops."

"Remember Klimov's murder?"

"Who can forget it, sir?"

"Klimov was director general of the Almaz-Antei Concern. They're the largest holding company in the defense sector. Taken out in a hit on the Moscow streets. It was an obvious mafia assassination," Pradischi decided.

"I've read the report, sir."

"Almaz-Antei have a monopoly in the area of producing and exporting state-of-the-art air defense missile systems. That's definitely an area the Mafia wants to get involved in. Then there was Sergei Shchitko, a commercial director of Ratep, an affiliated company to Almaz-Antei. He was murdered in Tokyo by an unknown assassin."

"And you think this is connected, sir?"

"The fact that Ratep produced electronic guidance systems for air defense systems makes me think they must be."

A tarty looking blonde left the club. At the door, she joked with the doormen for a moment, then walked off. She hurried to a tatty Lada, got in, and drove off. Pradischi quickly followed. They drove for a few streets to a rundown block of flats. Mischa got out the car and entered the flats. Pradischi parked in the shadows and waited a few minutes.

"Is that where she lives?"

Pradischi nodded. "She rents a flat. It's all part of her cover."

"How do you want to play it, sir?"

"We have to be careful. We can't afford to be seen. I'll park around the corner, somewhere secluded." Pradischi found a quiet unlit back street. "She's in grave danger. If Kranjenkov finds out she's a spy, he'll kill her."

"A gutsy lady, sir."

Pradischi nodded. "In Perm, she broke a child-prostitution racket being run from a children's home. She went undercover as a care assistant for six months. They had no idea she was a cop. She's a patient bitch."

"I don't know how she does it. She must be living on her nerves. She deserves nothing but our respect, sir."

"Stay with the car, Sergeant. We have to assume someone is watching her at all times. We can't afford to bulldoze in as a group."

Pradischi hurried to the front of the building, entered the ground floor, and was not surprised, in this hovel, to find the lift out. He walked slowly up the stairwell. The poorly lit stairs were a mugger's paradise. On the walkway close to Mischa's floor, he waited in the shadows, observing and noting his surroundings. When he was sure nobody was watching, he hurried along the landing to Mischa's apartment door and quietly knocked.

The door opened slightly while Mischa observed him. Happy, she opened the door. Pradischi slipped inside. As he shut the door, he noticed Mischa standing to the side, pointing a 5.45 mm PSM pistol at his chest.

"Lock and bolt the door," she ordered.

He did as requested, Mischa put the gun down on a nearby table.

Pradischi noted she had pulled the thick window curtains shut. "I'm glad you're not taking any chances."

"People who take chances in my line of work end up dead," Mischa stated coldly.

They sat in moth-eaten chairs. "Did you find out anything?" he asked.

"It's early days. I did manage to get in Kranjenkov's office when he was out yesterday. I've put a bug in his desk phone." She took out a small tape from a drawer. "Here's the first tape from the phone bug. I haven't listened to it. I'll leave that to you. You'll know what's relevant more than me."

She laid a tape recorder on the table and played the tape. There was a load of miscellaneous calls, until Kranjenkov rang England. He talked to Winterburn. The conversation became animated. "They'll be furious, Winterburn. You made a deal, you have to abide by it."

"I'm not stupid, Kranjenkov. This seems like a classic sting operation," Winterburn countered angrily. "Did you really think I'd just sit there and take it while you tried to con me?"

"Nobody is conning you, Winterburn. We know nothing about the missing money. We paid the bearer bonds via the courier as requested."

"The money isn't there."

"Nobody has set you up. It's dangerous to speak about this over the phone. I'll ring you in an hour on another line."

The call ended. Pradischi made some notes. "Excellent. We'll look into this Winterburn. The mafia are making a deal with him, so he must be a big UK player."

Someone knocked on the door. Mischa grabbed her

gun. She stared through the peephole, not recognizing Rominev. "I don't know him—you'd better take a look."

Pradischi had a look and angrily opened the door, dragging Rominev inside and shutting the door. "I ordered you to stay with the car, Sergeant!"

"It was urgent, sir."

"It had better be," Pradischi grumbled. "What could be so urgent it couldn't wait until I came back to the car?"

"This!" Rominev pulled a silenced Beretta from beneath his coat and shot them both. They fell to the floor. Mischa's head shattered as the bullet split her cranium and fatally lodged in her dura. Her gun clattered behind the table.

Wounded, Pradischi desperately crawled along the floor, trying to reach Mischa's gun. He almost reached it. Rominev smiled, kicking it away, and then fired a shot into the back of Pradaschi's head. The room was engulfed in the silence of death. Rominev momentarily stared at the grizzly scene then pocketed his Beretta and the tape and then departed.

His adrenalin pumped as he ran to the car. At the car, he sat and composed himself. Then he radioed in. "There's been a shooting—Mischa's apartment—I'm in pursuit of the attackers—" he stated nervously.

When control tried for further details, Rominev turned the radio off.

He drove onto the garden ring and then cut out to the suburbs and was soon out among the elite properties where the wealthy lived. The dachas of the former party apparatchiks were now owned by the super-rich of Russia's new entrepreneur barons. He stopped by a gatepost and pressed a button.

"Who is it?" a voice from an intercom asked.

"It's Rominev."

The electric gate started to open. "Drive carefully. There are dogs loose. Wait when you reach the house until security comes to meet you."

When the gates were fully open, Rominev drove in. As soon as he was in, the gates already started to close. In the shadows as he drove up the floodlit drive, he could see dogs darting about. When he reached the house, a man holding a dog whistle was standing on the steps. The man quickly beckoned Rominev inside. Rominev noted a CCTV camera following him as he mounted the steps.

Inside, an armed guard sat next to a table watching the screen for the CCTV set up. The guard stood up. "Follow me, please," he ordered.

They walked along an art-laden corridor until they reached a gleaming cherry wood door. The guard knocked firmly, waited a moment until he heard the call to enter. When it came, they entered. In the room, Russian Mafiosa, Chernekov's bulky figure was seated behind a huge Tsarist writing desk. Opposite him, on a red leather sofa, sat Kranjenkov.

"Go back to your post, Dimitri," Chernekov ordered. After the guard left, Chernekov asked, "Have you taken care of the problem, Rominev?"

"I've dealt with it, that's what you pay me for." Rominev stared at Kranjenkov. "They were listening to a tape recording of Kranjenkov talking to Winterburn."

"You fucking idiot!" Chernekov rounded on Kranjenkov. "You told me security at your club was fool proof. You assured me our dealings with Winterburn were in safe hands."

"My security is good. This was a momentary lapse," Kranjenkov said nervously.

Chernekov grabbed the tape and took it over to a technical set up in the corner. He put the tape in a tape recorder and played it. The conversation between Kranjenkov and Winterburn echoed through the speakers. "How could you let the police compromise you like this?" Chernekov asked angrily when it had finished playing.

Kranjenkov's face reddened. "I rang him back on another line, I take precautions—"

"Obviously, when one of your dancers is able to break into your office and bug your phone, you take elaborate precautions." Chernekov paused a moment to think. He turned to Rominev. "How many people know about this?"

"Captain Pradischi is dead, the undercover cop dancer is dead. I've removed anything incriminating from the murder scene. Once we've removed the bug from Kranjenkov's phone at his club, we should be in the clear."

"At least one of you is a professional." Chernekov stared angrily at Kranjenkov to emphasize his point.

Rominev took a notebook from his pocket. "Pradischi was taking notes. I found this notebook in his pocket. You now have all the evidence of the police's knowledge of the deal with Winterburn."

"Good, with security lapses like Kranjenkov's, I'm going to need it." Chernekov stood up and slowly paced the room. "Which leaves one more problem to take care of."

Chernekov nodded to Rominev. Rominev took his pistol from his coat pocket and turned it on Kranjenkov.

Kranjenkov stood quickly. "Please, there's no need for—"

Rominev fired twice at Kranjenkov's heart. A bewildered-looking Kranjenkov fell to the floor, his heart ventricles shattered under the bullet's impact. He was dead before he hit the floor. Rominev grabbed a thick cushion off a sofa, took a Beretta from his pocket, and placed the gun in Kranjenkov's hand, using Kranjenkov's hand to fire the Beretta into the cushion. He put the Beretta—the gun that killed Pradischi and Mischa—in Kranjenkov's coat pocket.

"We'll need this for ballistics," Rominev informed bewildered-looking Chernekov.

Chernekov was more bothered about the ruined cushion than Kranjenkov's demise. "You're the expert in these matters. We have to move fast. I want Kranjenkov's body out of here immediately, Rominev."

Chernekov pushed a button on the table. Two of his men appeared and removed the body. Rominev followed them outside and ordered them to put Kranjenkov's body in his boot. Rominev quickly got into Pradischi's car and drove off. He drove for a few kilometres until well away from the dacha. He stopped in a supermarket car park in a quiet corner away from any CCTV. Near a gaggle of foul-smelling bins, he lifted Kranjenkov's body out the boot and dropped it behind the bins.

Rominev cleared the area. When clear, he radioed in. "I've lost Pradischi's murderers. They drove down by the river, I skidded on some ice and they were gone. You need to instigate a search in the area of my last sighting."

Rominev gave them details, indicating the area around where he dumped the body. A search in daylight would find the body quickly. Rominev smiled, thinking happy thoughts, thoughts of the millions of roubles he'd made that would soon allow him to retire to somewhere warm and sunny.

He was close but he wasn't there yet. He'd worked too long as a cop to be naive about such things. If you got cocky, you made mistakes. He couldn't afford a mistake. If you wanted the perfect murder, get a detective to commit it, he thought, as he arrived back at the station and rushed inside.

In the detectives section, he was greeted by shocked

colleagues and received commiserative pats on the back from distressed cops. Rominev made all the right noises. He was already looking at retiring from the force through a stress-related illness. Tonight's events would help to highlight the problem. Tonight's events put him one-step closer to his goal.

Chapter 4

Hassan was shifty. McQuid didn't come to such a conclusion lightly. He had met many people in many strange places over the years and classed himself as a good judge of men after all his meetings with gangsters, corrupt politicians, and terrorist cells. It wasn't anything Hassan said. Hassan was always scrupulously polite, always seemed to be concerned about your welfare.

McQuid decided that Hassan was like the old Bedouins who offered hospitality when you entered their camp, yet the moment you stepped outside, they killed you. He sat on the tatty sofa in the backroom of the dark secluded Cairo coffee shop.

With his flaming ginger hair and freckles, he found the Egyptian autumn heat unbearable, and sweat poured down his back. He removed his robe and turban and laid them on the sofa.

"Sorry you have to wear this disguise, McQuid," Hassan apologized. "In recent times, government agents are everywhere. They're constantly waiting, watching, hoping we make mistakes."

"I've lived among the British and their spies. You've no need to tell me about security, Hassan."

After years as a member of the IRA, McQuid had been involved in all kinds of elaborate attempts at deceit in the name of security. That had been until the IRA had surrendered. The old leadership had shaken hands over the Good Friday Agreement. McQuid had been disgusted. The war could never be over until all Ireland was one. There could never be peace. He was now a member of the Real IRA, the only true Irishmen who'd fight to the death for a united Ireland.

"Have you made contact with the Russians?" Hassan asked eagerly.

McQuid liked to see the Arabs squirm. They were a volatile people, but they had their uses. "I have, but it's going to take time, Hassan. With so much at stake, we can't take chances."

"I know, my brother, the infidel devils wouldn't hesitate to kill us if they knew what we were plotting."

Hassan knew he was already on several international security hit lists. After Nine/Eleven, the CIA shot first and asked questions later. The Jews were no better. They had always had a shoot-on-sight policy toward Islamic fundamentalists. But McQuid had no doubt about his own people. "Our security is sound."

"I know." Hassan poured dark black coffee into glasses.

McQuid hated the stuff, along with the opium pipes regularly inhaled at the front of the café. In McQuid's eyes, drugs and security weren't good bedfellows.

"We need to finalize the deal. My backer is prepared to pay—" Hassan pressed. "—ten million dollars for the canisters."

"The Russians want fifteen million." McQuid found it hard to get his head around such figures.

"It's too much…how do you Irish say?…they're taking the piss."

McQuid would feel the same if he was Hassan. "I'm only the intermediary. I'm just the broker, relaying the price."

"It's too much. I need to negotiate, face to face."

McQuid smiled at Hassan. "I can tell you now, because of the current security situation, the Russians won't compromise themselves by meeting you."

"I need to see them in person. The extra money they require is too much. There has to be room for barter, a compromise to make the deal," Hassan grumbled.

"Let's talk straight, Hassan. My backers have their reasons for backing you, and it isn't just because of the money you pay. I can go back to them with your offer, but I'm warning you, as a friend, the price they've asked for they consider more than reasonable."

Hassan reflected. It was much more than he expected to pay. Islamic Jihad, with their rich oil sheikh backers, had the funds to pay such a price. They had the funds, but would they pay it? Hassan personally would have scuppered the deal, there and then, if the decision was his, but it wasn't.

"I thought the price had been agreed, and we were merely here to rubber stamp the deal."

"I'm sorry for any misunderstanding, Hassan."

McQuid shuddered for a moment when he thought about his vulnerability. He was taking a hell of a risk even coming here. It was a risk, but he didn't have a choice. The colossal shipment of arms the Russians were supplying to the Real IRA, for acting as intermediaries in their deals, made the risk worthwhile.

"Like you say, you're only the messenger." Hassan sighed. "If we agree on the fifteen million, how long until the goods are delivered?"

In the world of high-tech bugging devices, Hassan was careful not to give too much information away.

"You'll have them by the end of the month."

At least McQuid seemed to understand the need for speed, Hassan thought. "The delivery date is acceptable," Hassan said. "Please wait here while I talk to my colleagues."

Hassan left the room. McQuid sat, nervously waiting. He'd never trusted the Arabs. When they shook your hand in a friendly fashion, they were probably stealing your watch.

After a tense hour, Hassan returned. In his hand, he carried a Manila envelope, which he handed to McQuid. "My colleagues have agreed to the asking price. Inside the envelope, you'll find bearer bonds to the value of three million dollars. This is a down payment for the goods. Once the goods are on the way, further payment will be arranged."

"I need people to check the bonds first before the consignment is sent," McQuid said cautiously.

"Of course." Hassan expected nothing else. The Russian Mafia was infested with remnants of ex-KGB and were suspicious of everybody.

Hassan shook McQuid's hand, and McQuid put his disguise back on. The stench of the smelly bustling back streets wafted through his nostrils as they led him back to a side street near the Nile Hilton. He discarded his disguise in a rubbish bin, and, when he arrived back at the hotel, he was wearing his touristy slacks and shirt.

In his room, he examined the bonds without having a clue whether they were legitimate or not. Any thoughts of double-crossing the Russians he quickly put to the back of his mind. The Russians were evil bastards, and there'd be dire retribution for any treachery.

The Russians knew too much about the Real IRA's network in Ireland, could destroy the Real IRA in a matter of hours if they so desired. McQuid lay on the bed, savoring the joy of the air-conditioning. He didn't have any options. He'd have to fly direct to Moscow on the arranged flight. He'd follow the Russian procedure to the letter.

They had bribed all the right officials to allow him through the relevant customs points. That's why he liked working for them. They were pros, never made mistakes. He started to pack. In three hours, he'd be gone from this sweat-infested rat hole. Soon he'd be in Moscow—there, he'd really need to be switched on.

Chapter 5

The TGV train swished through the colorful French countryside. Sarah and Martin Appleton sat across from each other in the crowded compartment.

"Have you any idea what you're doing, Dad?" she asked, wringing her hands.

"Not really, love," Appleton admitted rather reluctantly.

It was too dangerous to stay in England. He'd told Sarah that he'd been greedily tempted to embezzle the money.

It was a half-truth. There were many reasons for embezzling the money other than plain greed. He decided not to burden Sarah with his problems.

She had been through enough already and badly needed a period of calm to rest and recuperate.

"When you stole the money, you must've had an escape plan," she whispered.

"Any plans I had have had to be changed. Your kidnap by Grimshaw and you killing him changed everything."

He was genuinely shocked that they'd gotten on to him so quickly. He'd planned to get Sarah out once the money was safely invested abroad. He thought he'd have a couple of weeks until it was discovered. The reality was that he'd only had days.

"We've both got new identities. We're safe for a while, love."

How could they ever be safe when they were dealing with psychos? Sarah thought. "Look what Winterburn's henchman did to me. He'd have killed me if I hadn't escaped. Is that what you call safe, Dad?"

"I thought I had more time, love. I didn't realize Winterburn would be on to me so quickly." He gently stroked Sarah's arm. "If I'd known he was on to me, I would've rushed to Cambridge to get you."

Sarah angrily pulled her arm away. "Sometimes you're so fucking stupid!"

They descended into reflective silence. The train raced on into the night. Sarah drifted off into tired, restless sleep. She didn't know her dad. Since her mother's death, they'd drifted inconsolably apart. Maybe when she woke up, this whole thing would have been just a nightmare.

Appleton waited until Sarah was asleep and then stepped out in the corridor. He took out his high-tech secure satellite phone. It had cost him a fortune. It was the same kind used by the CIA. He had to assume that Winterburn would have the equipment to trace incoming calls.

Winterburn answered on the fifth ring. When he realized it was Appleton, he immediately became attentive. "You realize that you're dead, Appleton." He paused for effect. "You know what a persistent bastard I am. It's only a matter of time before you make a mistake."

"When you found the money gone, this was obviously going to be your reaction."

"Then what's this call about?" Winterburn snapped.

"I called to warn you."

Winterburn laughed. "And what on earth do you want to warn me about? If you're ringing me to warn me about trusting shyster accountants who'll rob you blind, then I might listen."

Appleton sighed. "If you don't want to listen, I'll hang up."

"No, don't hang up," Winterburn pleaded.

Winterburn would have liked to cave the prat's head in with a claw hammer. Instead, he found himself pleading with the weasel for a few more minutes of conversation.

"I'll give you one last chance," Appleton said. "I want you to listen. Maybe it will save your life." Appleton gave Winterburn a moment to digest what he said. "The deal you've been working on with the Russians isn't what you think it is. They're not paying just to take over your empire. They've got a hidden agenda. I've looked into Kranjenkov and the Russian mafia big shots he's linked with, with the firepower and financial clout they've got behind them. If they wanted you blown away, they could easily do it. There was no need for them to pay you anything."

"Don't be stupid, Appleton. Nobody could take over my action without an army to back them up."

"They've got an army. After the breakup of the Soviet Union, there were many disgruntled Red Army soldiers and KGB operatives out there. A lot of them shifted over to the highly lucrative world of organized crime. There were billions of roubles to be made for people in the right place at the right time. Don't you think it strange that billionaire operators like the Russian mafia are interested in your shitty little world?

"My firms run half of London," Winterburn protested. "They want my empire because it's worth a small fortune. When we catch up with you, Appleton—"

"Believe me, I know what your boys will do to us if they find us. There's no need for graphic descriptions. I just wish you were my only concern."

"For the moment, I am."

"I'm more scared of the Russians than you, Winterburn."

"Well, you shouldn't be," Winterburn stated angrily.

"The Russians know they've got to find me. Through my research for you, I found out a lot about their operations. There's a lot you don't know, Winterburn. I'll give you one last piece of solid info before I go. You need to concentrate on the Russians."

Appleton hung up. He wondered whether Winterburn would take heed of his warning or not. With his wizardry with computers, Appleton had broken the Russian police computer codes. Appleton knew more about Kranjenkov and his associates than Winterburn would ever know. He'd broken the codes of the companies that Kranjenkov was involved in. His fluent Russian made all things possible. It had led him to a company called Armrotech Trading International.

Armrotech had some dubious Irish connections. There'd been some mysterious cargo shipments of motorbikes out of St Petersburg to Dublin. It was just after these discoveries, that security systems had jumped in and traced the leaks to Appleton. It meant that they thought that Winterburn knew about the mystery cargoes. It put Winterburn in as much danger as Appleton, but the fool didn't seem to realize.

Appleton had stolen the bearer bonds because he knew the Russians would be out to kill him. He needed to get out fast, and the bearer bonds were the only way of doing it. Without the bearer bond money, escape would be much harder. He sighed and then stepped back into the carriage.

Sarah was awake. "Where have you been?" she asked.

He sat back down. "I needed some air."

At the moment, he had no desire to argue with his daughter. This carriage wasn't a place for raised voices. Appleton was already planning accommodation. He had to stay one step ahead of his pursuers and keep his daughter safe. He only had his daughter's best interests at heart, but one look at her thunderous expression told him Sarah would never understand that fact.

For the moment, his daughter was an enemy, not an ally. She could never forgive him for almost getting her killed. He wanted her back, needed her reassurance, had a feeling they'd both need a lot of reassurance before this was all over and done with.

Chapter 6

Commander Andrievich was a big bear of a man. The small nature of his office made his seated figure seem even more imposing to a nervous, Rominev. Andrievich looked hard and long at Rominev, who was also seated.

"You need to put everything down, Rominev. This has the potential to be career destroying if you don't get this right."

"The events happened exactly as I said they happened, sir," Rominev stated. "Captain Pradischi and I waited outside Kranjenkov's club for Mischa to appear. We followed her back to her apartment. Pradischi was very cautious, insisted we parked well away from Mischa's apartment. He ordered me to wait with the car while he went to see her. I keep thinking back. If I'd gone with him to Mischa's flat, I might have prevented their deaths."

"Maybe, but you might've been killed along with them."

"It all happened so quickly, sir," Rominev stated. "It's hard to work out what did take place in that apartment. Pradischi was so careful with security. They wouldn't have opened that door unless they'd checked the person out first. The door wasn't forced, so it leads me to one conclusion, sir. I think that Pradischi knew the assassin."

Andrievich nodded. "It's possible. It would explain how the assassin managed to get inside the apartment without using force."

"As I said earlier, Pradischi had been gone a long time, too long. I sensed something was wrong. I decided to investigate. I went to the apartment block, and a man passed me on the stairs. At Mischa's apartment, I found Pradischi and Mischa's bodies. I confirmed they were dead, then I chased the man and radioed in the shooting." Rominev paused, momentarily holding his head in his hands. "He sped off in a car. I pursued him. It was dark. It wasn't long until I lost him. I trawled the streets for a couple of hours but he was gone, sir. So I radioed in and told them where I lost him."

"We checked out the number-plate. The Volvo belongs to a company that has a connection with Kranjenkov. The company said that the car was stolen yesterday."

"Well, they would say that, wouldn't they, sir?"

"I'm going to bring their people in for questioning," Andrievich stated.

There was a knock on the door and a young detective entered. "There's been a development. You'd better come quickly, sir."

They followed the detective to the incident room, where veteran cop, Sergeant Makelov, was waiting to greet them. "We've found Kranjenkov's body behind some supermarket bins. He's been shot twice with a PSM pistol. The crime scene investigators reckon he's been dead about five hours."

"In this freezing weather, it's going to be hard to ascertain an accurate time of death," Andrievich warned.

"We found a silenced Beretta in his jacket pocket. The officers at the scene reckon it could be the gun that murdered Pradischi and Mischa," Makelov stated.

Rominev laughed sarcastically.

"What's wrong?" Makelov asked.

"Don't you think that's a bit convenient?" Rominev said. "We find two officers investigating Kranjenkov's activities shot dead then, conveniently, we find the chief suspect for their murder dead with the murder weapon in his pocket."

"So you think it's a set up?" Andrievich asked.

"I think so, sir."

"It's possible," Makelov agreed.

"A classic fall guy," Rominev concluded. "What concerns me is, if someone set this up, then they must've had inside information."

They all reflected. There were always allegations of bribery and corruption about the police from the press.

Andrievich came to his own conclusion. "I want a tight lid kept on this. Anything any of you find out comes direct to me. If there's a leak, I'll know it's come from here," he warned sternly.

"We all want to find the killers, sir," Rominev said.

"I worked with Pradischi for ten years. He was a close friend. If anybody fucks up in this investigation, they'll have me to answer to," Malekov warned menacingly.

"We all want to find the bastards, Malekov. We'll all be careful." Rominev decided he'd have to be more careful than most.

"Very noble, Rominev, but it doesn't change one fact, and that is, that a cop in the Moscow division sold Mischa and Pradischi out."

The cops in the room looked at each other warily. This was the kind of mistrust and dysfunction Rominev was after. It gave him hope, made him realize that if he put enough doubts in his colleagues' heads, he could get through this.

Chapter 7

McQuid was bloody freezing. The temperature change was dramatic. A pudgy customs officer stopped him at a customs checkpoint. The officer ushered McQuid through a side door then led him along an icy corridor. McQuid knew better than to ask questions. He was shown through another door that led to the passenger lounge. When he turned around, the door had shut behind him and the custom's officer was gone.

McQuid walked casually across the lounge. As he approached the exit, a bearded man stepped alongside him. "Follow me, please."

Russian was McQuid's other language. He'd finished top of his class back at Trinity College. The IRA had taken note. With their regular dealings with Russian arms merchants, the IRA were always looking for believers who were multi-lingual.

Outside, McQuid was ushered into a waiting Saab. He stared at the terminal as he was driven away. The roof looked like it had been made out of thousands of flowerpots. In his eyes, it looked hideous. They passed the big square apartment blocks on the airport road. Snow flurries danced in the air. Snow could mask a multitude of sins, McQuid thought, remembering bodies they'd buried in the Irish countryside on just such days. They came to a halt in a slushy alley.

They got out the car and entered a restaurant's steamy kitchen. His chaperone led him past bustling kitchen staff cooking steamy meat in boiling pots. Off the kitchen, they stepped into a paint-flecked corridor. At the end of the corridor, the chaperone rapped on an office door, and they entered a poky office where mafia contact, Chernekov, alias Samutin, was seated.

Chernekov was a heavyset man with dark penetrating eyes. He told the chaperone to leave and then ordered McQuid to sit.

"I've got good news, Mr. Samutin," McQuid said. "They've agreed to pay fifteen million. They've also agreed to the shipment date." He handed Chernekov his briefcase with the bearer bonds inside.

Chernekov opened the briefcase and looked at them. After a few moments, he seemed happy. "You've done well, McQuid. We'll keep our side of the bargain."

McQuid thought of the AK-47s, the AKSU-74 sub machine guns, and the PSM pistols that would be shipped to them and had to suppress a smile. Since the Good Friday Agreement, the money had dried up from Irish sympathisers in America. The Real IRA had become outlaws among the Republican movement.

"If you ever need my services again, Mr. Samutin, I'm at your disposal."

"I'll bear that in mind." Chernekov picked up the phone and called a colleague. He finished the conversation. "I've arranged for a taxi to pick you up at the end of the alley you came in from. The taxi is driven by a friend. He'll take you to an overnight hotel. You're booked on a flight to Paris in the morning."

"It was nice doing business with you," McQuid shook Chernekov's hand and then left.

The hotel he was left in was grubby and in one of Moscow's seedier districts. McQuid wasn't surprised. In Moscow, you couldn't afford to be noticed, and he couldn't either. He was the linchpin keeping the Real IRA alive. He was the man that was going to make things happen. He felt like he was on the brink. When the arms arrived, his small band of followers would see he was the real deal, would see that the cause was worth fighting for.

McQuid wrapped himself in the faded sheets to keep out the cold. He was close now, within touching distance. He decided that, even in the cold and grime of this awful room, he'd sleep the best he had in a long while.

Chapter 8

Fordsham wondered why his boss wanted to see him. The first thing he noticed on entering Winterburn's office was that Winterburn was unusually jittery. "You wanted to see me, Mr. Winterburn?" he asked.

Winterburn nodded. "I want security tightened to the maximum. I want all the security cameras and alarms checked over in this place."

"Yes, Mr. Winterburn," Fordsham said and then left to carry out Winterburn's orders.

Outside, he noticed Winterburn's secretary wasn't at her desk. He saw steam still rising from a mug of coffee on her desk and decided she couldn't have gone far.

Eddie should have been on guard outside the door. Fordsham wandered outside and couldn't find him. It confirmed thoughts Fordsham had been having about Eddie lately. Eddie was getting too lax. Fordsham decided he would have to go.

He was already thinking about replacements. He had heard good reports about a couple of lads working for a minor East End firm and decided Eddie was about to be retired.

As he stepped back inside, Fordsham thought how

vulnerable they were at this moment to a rival's attack. It was then he noticed Kathy's feet poking out from a near-by sofa. He reached for his holstered Smith & Wesson and tried to fumble the pistol out of the holster.

Before he managed to, thudding bullets ripped into his chest, fired from a suppressed 9 mm MP5K-PDW sub-machine gun. Splintered bone decimated his lungs. Fordsham slumped to the floor, a cold maniacal death stare fixed on his face.

A ski-masked figure wearing leather gloves stepped out from behind a filing cabinet. He dragged Fordsham's body behind the sofa next to Eddie and Kathy's. The assassin moved stealthily along the corridor. He stopped for a moment outside Winterburn's office then, with a karate move, kicked the door in.

As the assassin entered the office, Winterburn fumbled to open a drawer, trying to grab a pistol. The assassin fired into Winterburn's shoulder, and Winterburn fell back over his chair onto the carpet. He edged toward the drawer.

"Don't be stupid, Winterburn," the assassin said in Russian-accented English.

Winterburn stopped and held his bleeding shoulder. "Whatever they're paying you to kill me, I'll pay you triple not to."

The assassin stepped around the desk. Winterburn smiled. He was shot up badly and resigned to his fate.

"Sit back against the wall," the assassin ordered.

Winterburn slid back against the wall. "I meant what I said, triple what they're paying you. All you have to do is let me disappear." He winced in pain. "They'll never know you haven't killed me—you could earn a small fortune by letting me go."

The assassin, Ilyich, known in the underworld as the Cobra, mulled over what Winterburn said. "I need to find an employee of yours. His name's Martin Appleton."

"I have a Martin Appleton working for me." Winterburn decided he had to keep the conversation going. If he could keep the assassin talking, then maybe there was a chance of making a lifesaving deal. "Appleton's a computer genius. He's always been too clever for his own good."

"I don't want his life history, just tell me where he is."

"Appleton's away on holiday at the moment," Winterburn lied. "I'll have to speak to my secretary to find out where he's gone to."

Ilyich shook his head. "Regrettably, your secretary is no longer available."

Winterburn thought of his secretary, Kathy, and their illicit affair that had been going on for years behind his wife's back.

"You need to quickly understand your situation," Ilyich continued. "None of your staff can help you now. You have one chance of survival, and that chance is if you cooperate with me."

"He's in France." Winterburn stated.

Ilyich looked hard into Winterburn's eyes. Winterburn didn't flinch. Ilyich removed a glass bottle from his pocket, on the side of the bottle was written: ACID. "I think you're lying."

Winterburn's terrified eyes engaged the bottle. "I'm not lying."

"Have you seen what this stuff does to skin?" Ilyich asked. "Any more lies and you'll get a practical demonstration."

Winterburn decided the Russians must know that Appleton had taken the money and fled. Telling the truth was his only option. "Appleton's stolen bearer bonds from me. He's fled the country with his daughter and my bonds. If you want the honest truth, I haven't got a clue where he is."

"At last we're getting to the truth." Ilyich started rummaging through the desk drawers with his free hand.

Winterburn noted that the gun remained fixed on him at all times.

"Were these bearer bonds he stole the same bonds that you claimed hadn't been delivered?"

Winterburn's face reddened. He stared blankly at the wall. The assassin was well informed, seemed to know all Winterburn's secrets. Winterburn tried to barter. "How much are they paying you to kill me?" Ilyich remained silent. "We could leave here and go to my home. My wife keeps a fortune in jewels in our safe."

"My employers want Appleton. If you could help me find him, I might reappraise the situation. If you helped me to find Appleton, then maybe their attention would be drawn away from you."

"Finding Appleton won't be easy. He's using an alias. I've got people on it—"

Ilyich held the acid bottle menacingly. "Tell me the alias!"

Winterburn remained silent. Once the assassin had the alias name, Brian Hopper, then Winterburn was dead. Ilyich flipped the acid bottle lid off. "Either talk or your face gets it."

Winterburn decided he didn't want to die a half man with an acid-burned face. "He's got a passport in the name of Brian Hopper, that's as much as I know."

Ilyich smiled. "You know what, this time I actually believe you, Winterburn." Ilyich drank the water out the bottle marked: ACID. "You see, Winterburn, people believe what they want to believe."

Ilyich fired a burst of gunfire into Winterburn's head. The bullets tore membranes apart before exiting and lodging in the wall's plaster. When the debris settled, Ilyich took an explosive charge from his pocket and placed it in Winterburn's lap.

As he exited, he placed further charges in the front reception where he'd dumped the three bodies. He removed his ski mask and put it and his gun inside a holdall he'd left behind the receptionist's desk. With the holdall on his shoulder, he calmly walked out of the building.

Outside, he almost collided with a UPS courier in the street. He barged past the courier and headed down a side street. When he arrived back at his car he'd parked in a nearby supermarket car park, he glanced at his watch. One minute to detonation. He started his car and drove off. When he was heading west away from Winterburn's office, he heard the dull thump of a bomb exploding. By the time he drove across Westminster Bridge, he could imagine the emergency services now descending on Winterburn's office. He'd made no mistakes, left nothing to link him with the murders.

His infallibility was why people employed him.

Chapter 9

Rominev enjoyed his visits to the bank. He had a safety-deposit box in the Anglo-American Bank in Central Moscow. The bank clerk put Rominev's box on the table then left the room. Rominev opened the box. Inside was Rominev's personal escape kit. There was a bankbook for Rominev's secret Cayman Islands account in the name of James Quigley, along with an American passport under the same name. It also contained a SIG-Sauer pistol and some cartridges, untraceable and purchased on the black market.

Out of his pocket, he took the recording tape and slipped it into the box with the others. It was a tape of a conversation with Chernekov concerning Kranjenkov's murder. Chernekov was lax around Rominev because Rominev was implicated in several murders. Chernekov obviously considered Rominev a safe person with whom he could talk freely.

Rominev would keep these tapes safe. He was compiling them as an insurance policy in case everything went wrong. He put everything back in the box and locked it. He pressed the buzzer to call the clerk and then he left.

Rominev was glad to get out of the stuffy bank. Bank

vaults with their claustrophobic atmosphere always felt like prisons to him.

A cold east wind ripped through him as he hurried back to his ice-covered car. He thought of those warm sun-kissed islands that awaited his retirement, and he couldn't wait. He was one big deal away from being wealthy enough to set up comfortably abroad and leave Russia for good.

Rominev had been heavily involved in getting the cargo on board the container ship. It was leaving St Petersburg for Alexandria then on to Haifa. Cherenkov was paying him a colossal sum for his help. Chernekov was his usual secretive self. He hadn't told Rominev anything about the deal he'd made with the Arabs.

Rominev radioed into control, saying he was now available after his private business. He was told to head to a biker's bar where there'd been a shooting. There were already uniforms on the scene when he arrived. Rominev nodded to them and they let him through the crime scene tape that had been hurriedly erected.

Inside the bar was Detective Victor Pavlov, a young good-looking detective from the station, slowly studying the crime scene.

"I've been very careful, sir." Pavlov said.

At least he'd been sensible, Rominev thought, noting the gloves Pavlov wore. "What have we got?" Rominev asked.

"There was a fight between two rival gangs," Pavlov stated. "Guns were drawn, shots were fired, and the dead biker on the floor was killed in the ensuing battle. There's blood leading along the street outside so we're sure that someone who fled the scene was wounded."

Rominev walked across the bar, taking in the dimensions of everything. He came to the greasy biker slumped dead over the dirty floor—a true Moscow gangland death, Rominev thought. Dying in a bar full of deadbeats in some meaningless biker conflict. He drifted outside where he found the barman and some other witnesses standing with a uniform.

Rominev spoke to the barman first. "The eagle and swastika logo on the victim's jacket, what's the name of the gang?"

"I wouldn't know," the barman said.

"So you run a bar that's a notorious biker hang out and, in all the times you've served these cretins, you haven't got to know the gang names."

"They're usually no trouble, Officer, they just drink and play pool."

"You've got a murder, people wounded—is that trouble enough for you?" Rominev snapped.

"We have the odd fist fight but I've never known a shooting," the barman defended.

Pavlov came over. "Well, you might not be forthcoming, but your barmaid told me that the dead guy belongs to a biker gang called 'The Disciples.'"

"Very strange, Pavlov, the barmaid knows all this, yet the barman who owns the place knows nothing."

"She must be more observant," the barman said.

"Or maybe she's not dealing drugs from behind the counter like you," Rominev said. His accusation was greeted by the expected silence. "I can make this as fucking difficult as you like. Do you want me to have this place raided every night? Do you want to be personally hounded all over Moscow by my colleagues?" Rominev let the barman think a moment. "There's an alternative. We're only interested in finding the murderer. I don't give a fuck about your sleazy world."

The barman weighed up his options. He was finding it hard to keep his bar afloat. Having the police hound him would finish off his business. The bikers were the bulk of his trade, and they would quickly shy away if the police kept raiding the place. People wouldn't come to him for drugs if the police were always hanging around. He decided cooperation was his only option. "And if I tell you everything I know, you'll leave me alone?"

Irritated, Rominev shook his head. "You don't get left alone, you just go low on the police priority list."

"There's also no comeback on your barmaid for talking to us," Pavlov said. "If I come back here and find she's being hassled—"

"She won't be. Just remember that I haven't killed anybody," the barman retorted.

"I'll remember it more when you've told me something I can use," Rominev said.

"The Disciples hang out in a club called, 'Metropolis,' out in the suburbs. They're led by Milo Vorolin. He was in here tonight with his men. Also, Prusentov, leader of the Brotherhood of the Motherland, was here with his boys. They were okay for a while, kept to their own business, then the arguments started. They argued over a girl, guns were drawn, and fired. When the guns were drawn, the entire bar staff ducked behind the counter. None of us saw much."

"Where do the Brotherhood of the Motherland hang out?" Rominev prodded.

"They don't come in here often. I don't know much about them."

Rominev decided the barman had given him all he had. He turned to Pavlov. "What do we know about these gangs?"

"Even the Communists had trouble with them, sir. They've been involved in criminal activities for years. Most model themselves on American biker gangs, lean to the far right," Pavlov explained.

"Any record of drug dealing?"

"Plenty, sir."

"You get back to the station and look into the two gangs. I'll hang around here and see what else I can get," Rominev said.

Pavlov left and Rominev went to interview bar trash. He looked at the dregs of humanity in front of him. There were drunks, druggies, and hags. The hags still thought they were lookers, even though their hard, lined faces showed their best years were well behind them. Rominev concluded that the sooner he was out of this jungle and in paradise the better.

Chapter 10

Appleton stared at the locked bedroom door. He banged on it and heard the sound echo in the silent house. "Come out, darling. I understand that you hate me, but sulking will get us nowhere."

Appleton wandered out onto the surfaced terrace, which afforded a wonderful view of the dazzling sunlit Mediterranean. Sarah had shut herself in her bedroom and locked the door after one of their many arguments. She was barely speaking to him, at the moment, and Appleton didn't blame her.

He stared down at the dense cypress trees and the cork oaks of the woodland below. The farmhouse was secluded. It gave them the hideout they needed. Hotels were too obvious and would be the first place that any pursuers looked for them. Staying at a hotel was a death sentence.

Appleton wandered back inside and was greeted by continued silence. He picked up his bankbook off the coffee table, looked at the name on the cover. He was now Brian Hopper. He smiled when he thought of the baffled look on the cashier's face when he'd handed her the bearer bonds to the value of ten million pounds. The manager had been called, they'd been led to an office. The bonds were taken away for verification.

"There are so many forgeries out there, Monsieur Hopper," the manager had announced. "A lot of them come from Eastern Europe."

Appleton was almost shaking with nerves in his chair. On the outside, he tried to show the calm demeanour of a legitimate businessman. The manager had informed him verification would take a few days and had given Appleton a receipt for the bonds. That was three days ago. By now, the bank would've determined whether the bonds were real or not. Appleton was shortly going to ring the bank to arrange an appointment to collect his money.

The bonds seemed real to him, but you could never be sure. Would the police be waiting for him at the bank if they proved to be forgeries? He had verified the bonds were legitimate with a banker acquaintance, though Appleton knew the acquaintance had gambling debts, so he couldn't be certain the acquaintance hadn't just told Appleton what he wanted to hear in order to get paid.

He rang the bank and arranged an appointment for early afternoon. In his bedroom, he lifted the drawer of a bedside cabinet out, hid his mobile phone beneath it. He'd banned Sarah from having a mobile, worried she might try and contact her friends.

Through friends, they could get to you. Through friends, if you gave them the opportunity, they could find you.

By hiding the phone, he was taking temptation away from her. He went to Sarah's bedroom and shouted through the door. "I've got to go to the bank, Sarah, I'll be back in two hours."

Sarah unlocked the door and came out into the hall. "I'll come with you," she said.

"It'll be safer if you stay here," Appleton decided.

"And what do I do if you don't return?"

"If I'm not back by the end of the afternoon, then you know something is wrong." Appleton took his wallet from his pocket. "There's a few thousand Euros in here. If you need to run, this'll get you a long way."

Sarah took the money and put it in her pocket. "I want to come with you."

"Not wise, love. They're looking for a father and daughter, they're not looking for a man on his own." Appleton hugged his daughter, was encouraged that she didn't flinch away. "What if the bearer bonds are forgeries? If they're forgeries, then the police might be waiting for me. You don't want to be standing there with me in the bank if the police arrest me."

"So you might not be back."

"I can't guarantee anything, love." Appleton didn't know what to say. He really had no idea what was waiting for him at the bank.

"After getting me into this mess, you'd better bloody come back and get me out of it," Sarah told him.

"Just sit tight and wait." Appleton kissed her cheek and then left.

Sarah drifted out onto the terrace and watched her father's hired car drive off. When she was sure he'd gone, she hurried to her father's room. She removed the drawer. She'd watched her father through the keyhole as he hid the mobile phone beneath it. She hurried out on the terrace and dialled a familiar number.

"Hello," her tired boyfriend, Jamie Pike, said.

"It's Sarah—"

"Jesus, Sarah! Where the hell have you been?"

"I've got problems," she confided. "I won't be around for a while."

"This is ridiculous. If you have problems, I can help

you. Where are you? I'll come and see you, help you sort it out."

In her mind, Sarah could see James's furrowed brow as he fretted about her troubles. "You can't come and see me—I'm not in Britain."

"My parents have just sent me some money for the new term. Let me come to you—"

"You can't come and see me, James!"

James sighed. "I thought you liked me, Sarah. We're meant to be a couple. Couples share problems. In times of trouble, they don't run away from each other. In times of trouble, you look to your partner for help."

"Trust me, James, it's safer if you don't get involved." Sarah couldn't stand the thought of James being in danger.

"Whatever problems you've got I want to be involved," he persisted. "I care about you, Sarah. I thought we had something special."

"It isn't that simple." Sarah decided it certainly wasn't. She was falling in love with her boyfriend. How could she ever run and leave James behind?

"It is simple if you make it simple."

Sarah weakened. She couldn't leave things with him like this. Even if it was just to say goodbye, she had to see him again. "If you come, you'll have to make sure you're not followed."

"Why would I be followed?"

Sarah found it impossible to explain over the phone. "If you want to see me, you do it my way, or we don't do it at all."

"Whatever you want me to do, I'll do, Sarah. I miss you, darling, I want to be near you."

"When I see you and tell you what's been going on, it'll all make sense."

"I hope so. I thought we had something going, Sarah,

I thought we had something and then you ran away.”

“I want you to leave Cambridge tonight, make your way to St. Charles Train Station, Marseille,” Sarah ordered. “I’ll meet you outside the main entrance tomorrow afternoon at three o’clock. Don’t tell anybody where you’re going, James. It’s vital you don’t mention this to anybody.”

“You’re frightening me, Sarah, you make it sound like you’re a secret agent.”

“Just do as I say! I’ll explain everything when I see you.”

Sarah hung up. Could she trust James to follow her instructions? He had to follow her instructions exactly. Sarah had seen, at close quarters with Grimshaw, what animals these people were.

Tomorrow she’d slip out early before her father was awake. She’d leave him a note telling him she’d gone to Marseille for the day. She’d worry about his reaction later. All she knew for certain was, after talking to James, she realized how much she loved him. James was her future. She’d decided that she couldn’t live without him and certainly couldn’t imagine any kind of future without James in it.

Chapter 11

Ilyich had Chernekov check Appleton out. Chernekov had come up with various addresses related to Appleton and his family. Appleton's Esher home was deserted. Ilyich had broken in, found out that everything was packed away, packed away in the way an owner did when he was going to be gone for a long time.

He headed to East Anglia. Appleton had a daughter at a Cambridge university. Although she appeared to have fled with her father, there was a chance she might've left a clue to her whereabouts behind. Breaking into her flat was easy. It was a cheap one-bedroomed flat, a typical student accommodation. Poorly furnished, cheap locks, and magnolia painted walls.

Systematically, he searched the flat, trying not to put anything back in a position other than where it originated. It was always better in such search operations that the occupant had no idea anybody had been there. He found no clue to her whereabouts. She hadn't left anything related to her father in the flat. He started to leave. At the front door, a pile of mail littered the floor beneath the letterbox. He slowly thumbed through the letters, all of them had stamps on, apart from an unstamped letter with just *Sarah* written on the envelope.

Outside in his car he opened it. The letter was a plea from a desperate boyfriend asking Sarah to contact him.

Ilyich smiled. The letter was a crack, allowing him to see a sliver of light through the doorway. If there was a boyfriend on the scene, then Sarah Appleton might try to contact him.

The boyfriend's name was James. A few enquiries and he found the boyfriend's full name was James Pike. Pike lived in nearby student accommodation. He was definitely worth a closer look. Ilyich would stick with Pike for a day or two just in case Sarah Appleton contacted him.

Ilyich sat outside Pike's flat. The boy appeared very early the next morning carrying a travel bag. The boy headed for the train station in a taxi. Ilyich followed, parked his car in the station's car park, and followed Pike onto the London train. The boy disembarked at Liverpool Street, got in a black cab. Ilyich got in the cab behind and told the driver to follow Pike's cab.

"Just like in the movies," the driver suggested.

Ilyich dangled a fifty-pound note in front of the driver, and then the driver was suddenly attentive. The taxi dropped Pike at Heathrow's Terminal 1. Ilyich paid his driver and followed Pike into the terminal. Pike had no idea that Ilyich was there. He wasn't acting like a man used to subterfuge.

Pike booked a ticket on the 10.00 Air France flight to Marignane International Airport, Marseille. Ilyich thought of Marseille and its sleazy underworld where anything was possible if you knew the right people and paid the right price. Ilyich decided Marseille was a good place for Appleton and his daughter to hide.

Ilyich booked a ticket on the same flight. There was still a half-hour until boarding. Ilyich made sure Pike was seated in the lounge waiting for his flight then stepped outside, where he rang his contact, Mr. Vaughn. Mr. Vaughn would be at the terminal before take-off, ready to take Pike's flight.

Ilyich had been too close for too long, tailing the boy. Even an amateur became wary if you stayed on their tail for too long. Ilyich would follow on a later flight. Mr. Vaughn was unshakeable once he was following you. Ilyich only employed the best. From the Cobra, the world expected nothing but the best.

Chapter 12

They entered the spotless house in the Moscow suburbs. The snitch had said the mafia used it as a cocaine storage house. The house was empty and someone had methodically scrubbed it clean. Makelov could see that they'd known the police were coming. They'd made sure they'd left no evidence of their presence in the house.

"They were tipped off," Makelov suggested after finishing the house search. He turned to his men. "Go over the place again, look under floorboards, everything!"

His men obeyed his orders. Makelov had already concluded it was a wasted act of bravado on his part. He stepped outside on the front porch. Rominev's car slid to a halt in the snow near the house.

Rominev was soon standing beside Makelov. "Well?"

"Nothing! I've got the men going through the place again, but they're unlikely to find anything."

"You said your snitch was reliable," Rominev reminded him. "There must be something in there."

Rominev pushed past an irritated-looking Makelov into the house. As Rominev surveyed the scene, Makelov was right behind him. They quickly came upon two forensic guys using dusting powder and brushes in a hunt for fingerprints.

"Have you found anything?" Makelov asked.

"I'm sorry, sir," the eldest forensics man said, "this place has been cleaned by professionals. We're unlikely to find a thing."

"Fucking brilliant!" Makelov snapped then strode back outside.

Rominev followed. "It's not their fault."

"Someone tipped them off, Rominev. If I find out who the bastard was, I'll gut them."

Makelov was a coarse man, Rominev had long ago decided. "Maybe your source isn't as reliable as you think."

Makelov shot him a dirty look. "My source is reliable. It's my colleagues that aren't."

The conversation lapsed into uncomfortable silence.

"Let's suppose that you're right—"

"I am right," Makelov snapped.

"So, you're saying, that someone inside the department is in the mafia's pay."

"I think tonight's disaster proves that beyond doubt, Rominev."

"You might be right. The way the house has been thoroughly cleaned leaves me in no doubt the mafia has used it to store drugs." Rominev stared hard at Makelov. "The fact that we haven't a clue who's passing information shows they're careful. Your suspicions about your colleagues are going to be hard to prove, Makelov."

"I'll prove it," Makelov promised.

"How?"

"I'll find a way."

Rominev didn't like it. Makelov was a bit of a dinosaur but he was a good detective. Surely, if he doggedly pursued it, then it was only a matter of time before Rominev appeared at the top of Makelov's suspect list. Rominev decided he would have to implement his retirement plan sooner than expected.

"Do you think this mafia snitch has got anything to do with Pradischi and Mischa's murder?"

"I've no doubt he has. Too much has happened on our watch lately for it to be anything other than an insider."

"Then I want the bastard more than anything, Makelov." Rominev gazed at the cold starry night sky. "I was close to Pradischi, he was like family to me."

"We'll get them, Rominev, they'll make a mistake, and then we'll get them."

Rominev wouldn't make a mistake. Now that he knew Makelov was on to him, he'd be doubly cautious. "So how do we corner the rat without them knowing we're on to them?"

"A good question. With infestations, you have to wipe out the problem at the source," Makelov suggested. "What we don't do is go shouting around the station that we think there's a traitor in our midst."

"So I'll have to be careful what I say."

"Not too careful, Rominev. If we're going to set a trap, then we'll need to provide some bait."

"So you want bait."

Makelov was suddenly attentive. "You've got something in mind?"

"I've been working on a biker gang murder. There seems to be a connection with drugs and some mafia contacts. I'm sure there's something from this that I can put out there that will grab mafia interest."

"That sounds like just what we need," Makelov said and then wandered over to talk to a forensics officer.

Rominev was pleased to be back in control. All he had to do was maneuver the situation like he always did.

Makelov played by the old rules, boringly predictable. Rominev was about to show him there was a new game in town.

Chapter 13

Pike stood outside the entrance to St. Charles Train Station at the arranged time. He glanced at his watch, it was just past 3 o'clock. Pike had done everything he could to make the meet, where the fuck was Sarah?

"Start walking, James," she said.

He couldn't see her. Then he noticed a girl in a dark track-suit and sunglasses strolling past. Sarah's jaunty walk was something she couldn't disguise. He fell in step beside her. For a couple of streets, he followed her in silence. They arrived at Sarah's hire car and got in. Just before they drove off, Pike leaned across and kissed her.

"I've missed you." They cuddled for a moment. "Why the need for all this secrecy?"

Sarah pulled away from their embrace. She started the car. "Let's get away from here, first."

She eased the Renault out into the traffic. They were quickly out of Marseille, driving along the coast. The cliff road, with its wild inlets plunging into the deep blue water of the shimmering sea, was a wonderful backdrop to their journey. Sarah found a quiet spot, pulled off the road, and parked.

They sat for a moment in silence. James watched a

distant yacht bobbing up and down as it danced through white-crested waves. He listened while Sarah explained the recent events in her life. James couldn't mask his expression of horror when she told him about killing Grimshaw.

"Because of Dad, we're now on the run," she stated. "I know Grimshaw was an evil man, but I keep seeing the face of that gorilla just before I killed him. I shouldn't have killed him—"

James held Sarah tight. "You had no choice. If you hadn't killed him, he'd have probably raped and murdered you."

"You're right, but that still doesn't make it easier. I killed a man, shot him in cold blood."

James pulled back. "This is mind blowing. How could that twat put you through this?"

She wouldn't rush to her father's defense. Twat was how Sarah saw him these days. She cried. James held her and kissed her.

"I'm in the second year of my degree, then I'm kidnapped and almost killed because of Dad's dodgy deals. When he tied me up on that bed at the caravan park, that bastard kept stroking my legs—"

James held her tight. "He's dead, Sarah, he can't hurt you now."

"If it were only that simple. You don't know these people, James, they're not the type of people to write this off to life experience. These are people who track you for eternity until you're dead."

"I'm here now," James tried to reassure her. He nudged her head beneath his strong shoulder.

Normally she'd have felt secure in his arms, but not now. Innocent James was no match for these violent psychopaths. By asking James to come here, she'd now put him in as much danger as she was. "Dad's going to be angry when he finds out I've brought you here."

"I don't give a fuck about your father," he said.

The smell of salt drifted off the sea, the sound of waves gently sloshed on the white sand. It was a beautiful place, James thought, a tragedy they were visiting it under such circumstances.

"I want to be back in Cambridge," Sarah said.

"I know," James reassured her. "Maybe one day this will be over and you'll be able to go back."

Sarah couldn't see such a day ever happening. "This nightmare is never going to end, love."

He agreed but decided it was best not to say so. "Where are you staying?"

"Dad's renting a farmhouse, we're out in the sticks." She pulled away from him. "He's going to be furious with me. This is his hire car. I left him stranded without transport when I sneaked off to meet you."

"So he doesn't know I'm here?"

"Of course not. If he knew I'd taken the car to meet you, he'd be furious."

"I came here because I love you," James admitted.

Sarah hugged him. "I love you, too, darling."

She got out the car, James followed. She led him down to the beach, could feel his hard phallus against her as he brushed into her when they lay on the sand. They made love in the quiet seclusion.

Mr. Vaughn eagerly watched the whole process through binoculars, loved it when his job had fringe benefits. As the girl pulled her boyfriend's penis inside her, Mr. Vaughn could feel his own manhood begin to rise. The joys of youth, he thought, as he took out his mobile to call Ilyich.

Chapter 14

In a booth in a quiet bar near the docks, Rominev slipped the envelope full of roubles into the harbor master's assistant, Boris Karishen's, eager hands. Karishen was a greedy man, Rominev had long ago decided Karishen had the pudgy features of a glutton, features that seemed to match his avarice.

"That's half the money, the rest will be paid on completion," Rominev said.

"There won't be a problem, nothing goes through St. Petersburg without me knowing about it," Karishen boasted.

"No mistakes," Rominev warned.

"Have I ever let you down?"

"There's always a first time."

An irritated Karishen shook his head. He had never let them down, didn't deserve the inquisition. He knew he was expensive but he was also reliable. "I'll need to know a week before when you want the container shipped."

"You'll have advance warning," Rominev confirmed.

Karishen stood to leave, Rominev grabbed his arm. "This is an important cargo, no mistakes."

Karishen wrestled his arm free. "Don't worry."

Karishen left. Rominev ordered a vodka then sat back in the booth. It was always best to wait a while after a meeting, take precautions. Chernekov wanted the consignment shipped in two weeks. A sealed container would arrive for loading on *SS Vladimar* setting sail for Haifa via Alexandria. They were shipping the consignment inside a container of tractor parts.

Rominev had already guessed what was in the container. It was probably weapons for Islamic extremists. Terrorists like Bin Laden came from wealthy backgrounds. They had the money available for all this shit. He didn't care what was being shipped to them. As long as Rominev got his cut, that was all that mattered.

Outside, the numbing wind seemed impossibly cold after the warmth of the bar. He pulled his coat tight and rushed to his car. He was quickly on the Moscow highway. He never met Karishen in the same place or at the same time of day. Rominev treated all his deals with the secrecy of a KGB spy operation.

The road was slushy, the traffic light, and the journey back to Moscow would be relatively stress free. He imagined the new life that awaited him in the South Seas or somewhere warm. Rominev thought of himself as a self-styled lord of the South Seas, marrying a teenage nymph who would see to his every need. When he left, he planned to take millions of dollars with him. He was thirty years old, planned to live a long time, and the lifestyle he intended to adopt wouldn't be cheap. He arrived back in Moscow at four in the morning. At a phone box near his apartment block, he stopped to make a call. He rang Chernekov on a secure number.

A tired Chernekov answered.

"The deal's set up. He just needs you to tell him when you want it loaded," Rominev instructed.

"Good, I'll finalize things later in the week," Chernekov said then hung up abruptly.

Chernekov was an ignorant pig, Rominev thought as he went back to his car. Chernekov's ignorance had the ability to get under Rominev's skin more than most people's. The problem was that Chernekov paid colossal sums for your services, money that Rominev was all too eager to take.

He'd killed for Chernekov on more than one occasion. It was an unbreakable link. Chernekov always had the threat of blackmail if Rominev didn't toe the line.

Rominev's apartment was the usual dishevelled mess. His work and his dodgy dealings meant he had no time to keep order in his home. His immediate problem was Makelov.

Makelov worried him. He was a good detective and could quickly bring Rominev's house of cards down. When Makelov latched onto an investigation, he was like a rabid dog who wouldn't let go. Rominev had limited options all the while Makelov was nosing around his business. Rominev had come up with a way of ensnaring Makelov. The barman Savian who owned the bar where the biker had been murdered had been a shady operator. Savian would be susceptible to pressure, Rominev decided.

He sat on his sofa, drinking vodka. The Makelov problem would have to be taken care of quickly, before Makelov got a foothold on what was going on. Rominev had so many problems and so little time to deal with them. If he stayed calm and kept everything under control, his South Seas life was there just waiting for him. It was there for the taking, and one thing was certain, at this stage of affairs, he could afford no errors.

Chapter 15

The moment Sarah walked into the farmhouse's living room, she could feel the tension in the air. Appleton's face was red. Her father's face always went a peculiar shade of red when he was angry.

"Where have you been?" he demanded.

"I left you a note, I told you I was going shopping."

"I don't for one minute believe you just went into Marseille to go shopping."

Sarah put the bags full of food and clothes down on the sofa. In the tight congested room, she could still smell James on her. She decided she need to quickly take a shower to get rid of the lingering smell of sex. "Believe what you like. You talk to me like I'm a prisoner, Dad."

Sarah went for a shower. Appleton was going to confront her further but decided he'd wait until after her shower. While she was in the shower, he unashamedly went through Sarah's bags and purse, looking for clues. He wasn't surprised when he found nothing. Sarah was a bright girl and, whatever she'd been up to, she certainly wouldn't have left evidence where he could find it.

Sarah appeared in clean clothes. "Did you find anything?"

"No." Appleton knew there was no point lying.

"And what did you expect to find?"

"I don't think you fully understand the danger we're in, Sarah. One slip up with these people after us, and we're dead."

"After almost being raped and murdered, I think I fully realize the danger I'm in, Dad."

Appleton sat on the sofa. "Your kidnapping showed you how dangerous these people are. We only need to let our guard slip once, and we're finished."

Sarah sat on the sofa next to him. "What a mess."

"I'm sorry, darling." Appleton thought about his stupidity, cursed the day he'd ever met Josh Winterburn. "When I was having money difficulties, a colleague put me onto Winterburn who would pay good money for my services, the colleague said. One thing led to another. I quickly found myself caught up in Winterburn's seedy world. When the Russian deal came along, I could see a way out, a chance to make the big financial killing that would allow me to escape Winterburn's clutches."

"And you never thought about the danger to me?"

"I thought about it. I miscalculated. On Winterburn's calendar he was meant to be visiting his brother in Leeds for a few days. I thought I had time to flee with you before he ever discovered the bonds were missing."

Late for birthdays, always late with her Christmas presents, hoping to pick up something cheaper in the January sales, Dad really was a shit, Sarah thought. "You shouldn't have involved me in this fucking mess!"

"You made a call! I was looking at my phone while you were out. You made a call to Cambridge yesterday."

"Is this on the phone I'm not supposed to know you have?"

Appleton was irritated she'd found his phone. "That's the one."

"Of course, now I'm your prisoner, I'm no longer allowed any contacts with friends."

"Who did you ring, Sarah?"

"Just a friend."

"Does this friend have a name?"

Sarah saw no point in lying. "His name's James, he's my boyfriend."

Appleton sat and thought. She'd rung this boy yesterday, had sneaked out this morning, and taken the car. A horrible thought suddenly registered. "Please tell me you didn't meet this boy when you went to Marseille today."

"His name's James, and I love him."

"So you met him."

"Why should I deny it? I needed to see him."

Appleton couldn't believe it. "We have to pack."

Sarah grabbed Appleton's arm, "I'm not going anywhere."

"If they followed him, they could be onto us."

Appleton couldn't believe she could be so stupid. He pulled his arm free and started to get their things together.

"They wouldn't have been able to follow him. After I called, James left immediately for France. If someone followed him, he'd have noticed them."

"You don't notice these people, Sarah. If he was followed, he wouldn't know."

"I'm not going anywhere without James."

"We have to get moving—"

"I'm not going anywhere unless James comes with me," Sarah insisted.

"Be reasonable, Sarah—"

"If you won't let James come with us, then you're going on your own."

"You can't stay—it's too dangerous!"

"And what's your alternative, Dad? A soulless,

friendless, existence. A life always on the move, scared to make any friends."

"At least you'll be alive."

"This isn't really living, is it, Dad?"

Appleton couldn't agree with her more but what else could he do? "Maybe your boyfriend won't want to go on the run with you forever."

"He loves me. He'll come with us."

"And where is lover boy now?"

"He's staying in a hotel in Marseille. If I ring, him he can be here within the hour."

Appleton sighed, reluctantly handed her his mobile phone. "I assume you know his mobile number."

Sarah smiled. At last she could see a chink in her father's armor. If James fled with them, then maybe there was a chance for some kind of life for her. James sounded sleepy when he answered his phone. Sarah told him to take a taxi to the farmhouse. After James had noted the address, Sarah hung up.

James, in his hotel room, nervously put his mobile phone down. "I did what you told me."

"You've done well, boy, now give me the address," Ilyich ordered, pointing the silenced Beretta at James's chest.

James handed Ilyich the address. Ilyich took the address and smiled.

"Don't hurt her," James pleaded. He looked at the Russian's cold dark eyes and had no doubts the man was a killer.

"You've done well, boy, it's nice to meet a young man who can quickly grasp the situation." Ilyich fired the gun twice into James's heart, fatally ripping apart the ventricles.

James died with a horrified expression on his face. After the body had settled, Ilyich dragged it over to a nearby wardrobe and dumped it inside. He put the address in his pocket. It was the same address that Mr. Vaughn had given him when he'd met him in the hotel car park.

Ilyich was closing in. Chernekov wanted them dead. Ilyich had a different agenda. Killing them could wait. Ilyich wanted some of the money Appleton had stolen, and to get to that money, one thing was certain, he had to take Appleton and his daughter alive.

Chapter 16

Savian sat in his poky office at the back of the building that housed his bar. Rominev sat opposite.

"Do you know how to kill a man, Savian?" Rominev asked, not sure what to make of the shifty bar owner.

"I've killed before," Savian ventured. "I was a conscript in Afghanistan, had to kill to survive." He took a large gulp of vodka from his glass on the table. His attention momentarily drifted, and he had a flashback to the horrors of that awful war. "You could say that I'm a war hero. As a war hero, my reward for showing bravery in battle and serving my country is to be continually hounded by the Moscow Police."

Rominev smiled. "This isn't hounding, Savian. If you want hounding, then that can be arranged. Let's just call this a friendly visit, soldier."

Savian guessed where this was leading. "How much do you want and when do you want it paid?"

Rominev shook his head. "Don't insult me, Savian. Is that what you think I am—a cop on the take?"

"I don't know what you are, Sergeant, and I have no idea why you're here?"

"This isn't about money, Savian. This is about another matter that could be of mutual benefit to both of us."

"Just tell me what you want, Sergeant." Savian was tired of all this shit. The only constant he seemed to find when he had dealings with the authorities was that they were all corrupt.

"I need your help, Savian. I need you to help me with a set up," Rominev stated. "I want you to ring me when one of the biker gangs is in here."

"In here? Why would any of them come back here after the shooting?"

"They'll come back because you'll invite them back," Rominev explained.

Savian's face was masked with horror as he thought about the possibility of a gang war in his bar. "Don't ask me to do this."

Rominev refilled their glasses from the vodka bottle on the table. "You were a soldier in Afghanistan. You were surrounded by death. A few more deaths shouldn't be a problem." Rominev decided to add a sweetener. "There's also $50,000 for you if my scheme's successful."

"And what if it fails?"

Rominev smiled. "If it fails then, regrettably, I'll have to kill you."

Savian decided a man so devoid of emotion as Rominev would definitely carry out the threat. He surveyed his options. He didn't have any. Savian came to a decision. He wasn't sure what Rominev wanted of him, but, whatever it was, it was going to be bad. "And what happens after?"

"When it's over, I'll pay you the money, make it known that you're my snitch, and make sure that you're left alone by my colleagues."

"It sounds so simple, Sergeant."

"It sounds simple because it is."

"And how do I know that you'll keep to your side of the bargain?" Savian pressed.

"I'll have to, because once we've committed the crime, we'll both be inexplicably linked."

Savian didn't trust him. Rominev was a snake. But Savian didn't have a choice. Rominev had made sure he didn't. "When do you want to do this?"

"One week from today. I'll ring you in a few days and make sure you're ready."

"What if I can't get hold of them in a week?" Savian protested.

Rominev wasn't listening. "Just do as you're told."

With that, Rominev left Savian cuddling his vodka bottle. As he walked to his car, he wondered how reliable fear would make Savian? He'd intimidated the man, let him know what awaited failure. Whatever Savian thought, it didn't matter, as necessity brought together the strangest bedfellows.

Chapter 17

There was a knock on the farmhouse front door. Appleton immediately tensed. He hadn't heard a car, hadn't heard anybody approach the door.

"I didn't hear a taxi arrive," Appleton said.

"An assassin wouldn't walk up to the door and knock, Dad."

"Go and look out the window," a jittery Appleton ordered.

Sarah looked. She couldn't see James's face but it was unmistakably the black Reebok baseball cap and gray jacket of her boyfriend. Sarah rushed to the door and opened it. A strange man wearing James's clothes stood before her.

Apart from the pale lifeless skin of the man's lined face, she also noticed the silenced Beretta in his right hand.

"Step inside—slowly," he ordered.

Sarah edged back nervously. Appleton saw Ilyich with the gun pointed at Sarah.

"Sorry, Dad," she said.

"Both of you put your hands on your heads and stand against the wall," Ilyich ordered.

"We've hardly any money—"

"Stop it, Appleton. You know I'm not a thief. You know why I'm here."

Ilyich noted the look of defeat on Appleton's face. Over the years, Ilyich had seen that look on many men's faces when he cornered them. He frisked them, Appleton was relieved he'd left his phone in the bedside cabinet and not in his pocket.

Sarah looked at James's clothes the man was wearing, "Where's James?"

"Regrettably, he didn't make it," Ilyich stated coldly.

Sarah flung wildly at him. Ilyich diverted her lunge and cracked her over the back of the head with his gun butt. Sarah fell to the floor, unconscious. Appleton started to move and quickly stopped when he saw the Beretta now pointing at him.

"Don't be silly, Appleton," Ilyich said. "She's only unconscious."

"Why did you need to kill him?" Appleton asked. "He was just a student. He wasn't involved in any of this."

"You killed him, Appleton. If you'd never gotten involved with Winterburn, then he'd still be alive."

"Leave Sarah alone. She knows nothing of any of this," Appleton pleaded.

"My employers want the bonds you stole back," Ilyich stated. "They also want to know how much you know about their operations."

Appleton could see he had nowhere to turn. "If you spare my daughter, I'll give you everything."

Ilyich laughed. "You're in no position to bargain, Appleton."

"She doesn't know anything."

"Obviously, you're going to tell me that."

"She thinks I've just stolen money from Winterburn and you're after me for that."

"Money is the last thing concerning Winterburn now," Ilyich stated coldly.

Appleton decided that Winterburn was dead. Appleton didn't know where that left him. "So the moment I hand over the money and you get everything you want, you'll kill us both."

Ilyich smiled. "Maybe, and then maybe I don't always do what I'm told."

You had to offer them hope. This was something Ilyich had quickly learned in his early days. Without hope, he had no chance of Appleton's unforced cooperation.

"If you let my daughter go, I'll tell you everything."

"You're in no position to bargain, Appleton. I was an expert knifeman in my Spetsnaz days, I could make you talk in minutes." Ilyich paused a moment for impact. "If I set to work on your daughter—"

"There's no need. Let her go and you have everything," Appleton stated. "The bonds have been cashed. The money is in an account under my new identity. Only I can get access to that account."

"Just sit on the sofa and relax—"

"Can I lay my daughter on the bed?"

Ilyich looked at Sarah, unconscious on the floor. "Why not?"

Appleton carried his daughter to his bedroom and laid her on his bed. Ilyich checked that the window was locked and then locked the bedroom door.

Back in the living room, Ilyich made Appleton sit on the sofa. "You're a computer financial expert, Appleton. How do I come out of this whole adventure with a retirement fund of one million dollars without my employers ever knowing I've got the money?"

Appleton at last saw a chink—greed. Greed was good, especially when you were fighting for your life.

Appleton decided that if Sarah had any chance of survival. he had to give the sales pitch of his life. Any deal he made with this assassin had to be watertight, had to ensure Sarah's survival.

Chapter 18

Sarah awoke, dazed and confused. She reached across for her lover, but James wasn't there. Her head felt like a sledgehammer had hit it. The sun glared in her eyes from the west facing window. As her head slowly started to clear, she realized it had to be late afternoon. Suddenly, she remembered the blow to her head, filling her with horror as she knew James was dead.

Tears ran down her face. The monster who'd hit her had killed James. She tried to sit up but a violent pain in her head made her lay back down. The sheet was blood stained from her head wound. She moved her head onto a clear patch.

She lay there, quietly listening, could hear her father talking to the monster in the living room.

She tried to get up. She raised her head up slowly, maneuvered her body to a seated position. She sat on the edge of the bed a moment, gathering her thoughts. When she was steady, she went to the door and window and tried them both. They were both locked. She was in Dad's room. She rushed over to the cabinet and was relieved to find his mobile phone still there. She called the police, whispering in her excellent French, and explained the situation.

They told her to remain calm, a SWAT team was on the way. She stayed on the line and barricaded furniture in front of the door. She had to keep the Russian out until the police arrived. There was nothing she could do about Dad, other than hope, the police could storm the farmhouse without killing him.

Soon a pile of furniture was wedged against the door, making it impossible to push the door open. She pulled the mattress off the bed and used it as a shield against stray bullets. She lay beneath it as a shelter. All she could do now was wait. Wait and pray.

Chapter 19

Appleton looked into the Russian's cold eyes, not sure whether the man was buying it. "If you let me handle things the way I explained, then I guarantee your employers will never know anything."

The Russians weren't stupid. When Ilyich turned up with a shortfall, they were sure to be suspicious. Appleton decided that bullshit was the only way to buy time.

"You make it sound simple, Appleton. We both know it isn't that simple. In Russia, to reach the top in the underworld, you have to be intelligent and ruthless. Whatever scheme you devise has to be fool proof."

Appleton didn't know whether that meant the Russian was interested or not. He hadn't cut Appleton up yet. At least, that showed he was still listening. Appleton needed to stall—buy time to think of a plan. "Could I check on my daughter?"

Ilyich decided to let him. If he was going to get anywhere with Appleton, he'd probably have to torture the man's daughter. For that, he needed her to be alive.

Appleton unlocked the bedroom door and tried to push it open. The door was jammed. He couldn't move it. He pushed hard but the door wouldn't budge.

Ilyich tensed. "What's going on?"

"The door's stuck. I can't open it."

"Lie face down on the floor with your hands behind your head," Ilyich snapped.

Appleton did as ordered. Ilyich shoulder-charged the door. It moved slightly but he quickly realized it was blocked with furniture. "If you've got any sense, young lady, you'll move whatever's barricading the door." His order was met with silence. "Do you want me to shoot your father?"

Outside, Ilyich heard footsteps on the gravel. He looked out a window and saw armed police surrounding the farmhouse. He kicked Appleton hard in the ribs. "Get up!"

A stunned Appleton got sluggishly to his feet. Ilyich led him along the passage to the living room. From a cocktail cabinet, Ilyich tipped bottles of booze over furniture. He took a lighter from his pocket, clicked it alight, and threw it on the floor. Red-blue flames licked across the carpet, igniting furniture.

Appleton tried to push past Ilyich to save his daughter, Ilyich karate chopped Appleton on the neck, and Appleton fell to the floor. Ilyich levelled his gun on Appleton. Appleton heard shots. He hadn't been hit, but Ilyich fell forward, his body riddled with gunshot wounds. He died on the carpet. Policemen in flak jackets were suddenly upon Appleton.

"My daughter's in the bedroom at the end of the corridor," Appleton pleaded as the racing flames engulfed the dead Russian.

"We'll get her out through one of the windows," a policeman said in English as they dragged Appleton outside.

On the gravel drive, a dazed Appleton could see his daughter being lifted out the bedroom window. Sarah must have used his mobile to call the police, had saved both their lives. He owed his daughter everything and realized he'd given her nothing but misery. They both clutched each other in a nearby ambulance, and Appleton's tears began to flow as he thought of the misery he'd caused her.

Chapter 20

The docks were quiet and still this early in the morning. This was just how the lorry driver Vassily liked it. He'd been ordered by his employers to arrive at the dock gates before dawn. The customs officer who attended him pretended to be going through the motions of checking the container. Reality meant he barely gave the container a cursory glance. After twenty minutes, the container was cleared. Vassily crunched the gears and roared the lorry over to the loading bay.

Karishen stared at the scene from his dock office close to the loading bay. Until the container was actually loaded on the ship, he wouldn't relax. Once the ship sailed for Egypt, his responsibility ended, and he wouldn't be blamed for any failure that then occurred.

Karishen already had plans for the money he'd earned for getting the cargo through. He'd promised to take his mistress, Natasha, on a shopping trip to Helsinki while Karishen's wife was away visiting her sister in Moscow. He could feel his penis awakening when he thought of young Natasha in her silky black stockings in a Helsinki hotel room awaiting his attention.

The money he received from this job would allow him to buy Natasha expensive presents. Karishen liked providing his mistress with gifts and exciting trips, all the things boys her own age couldn't give her. An hour later, when he saw the crane gently easing the container on board the freighter, it brought a smile to his face.

He booked tickets on an Aeroflot Helsinki flight for Friday evening. On the way home, he stopped at a payphone and rang the number he'd been given to confirm the cargo was safely on board. Thoughts of Natasha distracted him on the drive home. So much so that he didn't notice the Volkswagen two cars back following him.

When Karishen entered his home, the Volkswagen parked up the street. Inside the car, Chernekov's men, Valerentov and Alexanski, stared at the house.

"Karishen is a buffoon," Valerentov said.

Alexanski decided that Valerentov's puggish features looked exceptionally scary when caught in the glow of a nearby street light. "Can't we just kill him now and save all the bullshit?" Alexanski asked.

"We kill him after the ship's sailed."

"I'm only trying to make our lives easy."

Alexanski always tried to cut corners. Valerentov would stick exactly to the timetable Chernekov had given them. Valerentov was loyal to his mafia boss, who paid him a fortune, and Chernekov's money bought unquestioning loyalty.

"We stick exactly to the timetable," Valerentov ordered.

Alexanski took one look into Valerentov's cold, hard eyes. Valerentov was a man you dared not argue with, because Valerentov was a man Alexanski had personally seen kill many times with his bear-like hands.

Chapter 21

Appleton was sitting next to his solicitor, Carlton-Price, in an interview room in Paddington Green police station. Opposite sat DCI Tony Rowland and his assistant DI Alan Wright.

"We've established that you worked for Winterburn, Appleton," Rowland stated. "As you've been informed, Winterburn and some of his staff were murdered in their Docklands offices last week."

"I'll take your word for it. I haven't spoken to Winterburn in weeks."

"We've established that my client was in France when these attacks took place," Carlton-Price said. "I hope you're not suggesting he was involved."

"Somebody killed them. Your client had recently fallen out with Winterburn," Rowland said.

"My client has no experience with guns. I've read the report, the murders that took place at Winterburn's offices were carried out by ruthless killers. You can't believe that my client did this."

"I'm not saying Appleton killed them. In light of the fact that your client stole millions in bearer bonds from Winterburn, and Winterburn was after him, your client had every reason to want Winterburn dead."

"My client is a thief, not a murderer, Chief Inspector."

"We've established his theft," Rowland informed him. "The French have found $9,915,000 in this false account in Appleton's alias. With that amount of money, your client could easily have hired assassins to kill Winterburn."

"And what about this Russian sent to kill my client? Surely, this Russian is more likely to have been involved in the murders than my client."

"Unless your client is more forthcoming, then he's going to prison for a long time, Mr. Carlton-Price. Winterburn was dealing with the Russian mafia. Your client stole money from Winterburn. Winterburn and his office staff are dead, murders your client could have ordered. If your client's got anything to say in his own defense, I suggest he says it now."

"Can I speak to my client alone for a moment, Chief Inspector?"

"You can talk," Rowland said. The detectives turned off the tape and left the room.

Carlton-Price turned to Appleton. "We have to give them something, Martin."

"I wasn't involved in any of the murders."

"Things aren't that simple, Martin."

"If I snitch, then I'll need police protection. If I snitch, then Sarah is going to need police protection."

"If you don't give them something, you could be facing years in prison," Carlton-Price warned.

"And what about Sarah? She was dragged along through all of this by me. She is innocent of everything," Appleton stated.

The police seemed to know nothing about Sarah killing Grimshaw. Appleton decided it was definitely something he had to keep quiet about.

"I'll do my best for Sarah. At the moment, she's refusing to say anything to the police."

"And if I deal with the police, what's in it for me and Sarah?"

Carlton-Price didn't know. He had no idea what Appleton had, so he couldn't make any promises. "Tell me what you've got, and I'll be able to make a judgement."

Appleton leaned back in his chair and told Carlton-Price how he'd stolen Winterburn's money and what the money was for. Carlton-Price took notes. Appleton didn't care. He had to make some kind of deal that would save Sarah from prison. Things had gone beyond the stage of secrecy.

"And you can prove the Russian mafia was involved in all of this."

"I can prove it. I can give them the names of Russian kingpins, all the evidence is in a safety deposit box. This is my insurance policy."

What would it insure? Carlton-Price had no idea. It at least gave them something to deal with. With what Appleton was facing, the more they had the better. "You want to try and deal with the police?"

"There's no other alternative," Appleton said.

He was right, Carlton-Price thought. There was no alternative but to try and make a deal while they had something to give them. If events changed rapidly, and the information Appleton had wasn't needed, then they had nothing. Carlton-Price called the police back in. They'd make a deal quickly.

Chapter 22

Savian had called. It was time. Rominev left his half-eaten omelette on the table in what he laughably called a kitchen in his cramped apartment. He parked his car a couple of streets from the bar and walked the rest of the distance through snow-dusted alleys. Under his thick leather coat, he had a Walther PPK pistol and a Micro-Uzi. The Micro-Uzi had cost him a fortune on the black market.

As he approached, he saw the gang's trademark Suzukis and Yamahas parked outside the bar. He paused near the entrance, composed himself for what lay ahead. He stepped into the bar and hostile stares from bikers greeted him. Rominev ignored them and went to the bar. There, he bought a beer. Savian barely spoke to him when he served him. Savian's nonchalance would be irrelevant once it all kicked off, Rominev decided.

The bar had its usual assortment of deadbeats littered around dusty corners. There was a group of loud-mouthed bikers seated around a table. It was three weeks since the shooting, and Savian had managed to entice them back.

Rominev spotted their leader, Prustenov holding court. Rominev stood drinking for an hour. The bikers were drunk, the witching hour was almost upon them. Rominev stepped out of the bar for a moment and made a call. Makelov answered on the third ring.

"It's Rominev, I've uncovered a lead," he explained. "I might have discovered the spy in our midst. Remember that biker shooting at Savian's bar the other week?"

"Of course," Makelov said.

"I need you to come to Savian's bar immediately."

"Why?"

"I found the rat, he's in here, Makelov. I can't talk now, just get down here." Rominev hung up.

Makelov would be there in ten minutes. He would be unable to resist the bait.

Rominev looked around him in the empty street. Flecks of snow gently buffeted his face. The witching hour was now. He took a ski mask from his pocket and slipped it over his head. As he stepped back into the bar, he gave Savian a nod. Savian ducked behind the heavy cherry wood bar.

A heavy metal track thumped from the jukebox. Rominev slipped the Uzi out from under his coat and fired a burst at the bikers. Glass and flesh shattered, blood splattered.

Rominev ignored the dead bikers and turned the Uzi on the other half of the bar. The drunks scattered, but the numbing effect of the booze meant they moved too slowly. Rominev changed the magazine just in time to shoot the last survivor heading for the exit.

ACDC came to a grinding halt as bullets severed jukebox wires. Rominev stood a moment, contemplating the eerie silence. An angry Savian leapt up from behind the bar, his face angrily reddened as he observed the carnage.

"You said you were only going to kill the bikers," Savian protested.

"So I did," Rominev said.

He fired one final burst of the Uzi into Savian's chest. The burst splintered wood and smashed glass, ripping through Savian's bone and flesh.

Savian gave Rominev that look. The look you saw on all these reptiles' faces when they realized you were a bigger shit than they were. Rominev walked past the bodies, undisturbed by his actions. There were no witnesses. He still wore the gloves he'd worn since entering the bar. He went and stood by the entrance, Makelov must be almost there.

Chapter 23

Makelov's car slid to a halt in the snow on the opposite side of the street to Savian's bar. He spotted the bikes parked outside. He couldn't see Rominev's car. That didn't mean anything. Rominev was a cautious motherfucker. It didn't mean he wasn't in there. He zipped up his coat tighter to keep out the cold. Only drunks and cops were stupid enough to be out on a night like this. He crossed the road keeping out of the streetlights and in the shadows. The bar was very quiet—too quiet, he decided.

Through the grimy windows, he could make out people but no movement. An agitated Rominev suddenly appeared out the shadows.

"Thank, God!" Rominev said.

"What's wrong?" Makelov asked.

"It's bloody mayhem inside—I've called it in. units are on their way." Rominev stepped inside.

Makelov followed. Makelov was stunned when he observed the mayhem. "Jesus!" he said.

Rominev stepped back a yard and let Makelov drift past him. "It's some kind of bikers' war. The customers got caught in the crossfire."

Makelov examined some of the dead. "This is bloody

awful." Something suddenly registered in Makelov's brain.

Rominev could see the moment. Makelov stopped examining the dead. "What's this got to do with the spy in our midst?" he asked.

As Makelov turned to face Rominev, he saw the Walther PPK pointing at him in Rominev's steady hand. The gun clarified everything, a cold realization that he'd been set up. Rominev fired three times at Makelov's abdomen, ripping it to pieces. Makelov dropped to the floor, his face etched with horror. He died in a pool of blood next to the bikers. As Makelov died, Rominev concluded that Makelov's kind of policing had been dead for a long time.

There was no CCTV. Shit holes like Savian's place never had such luxuries. Rominev slipped out the door and rushed back to his car. He was back in bed soon after. When his phone rang at three in the morning, he acted shocked by the news of the shootings.

At Savian's bar, he found police cars, ambulances, and a cordoned off crime scene. He was ushered through the crime scene tape by a uniform and shown to the horror inside the bar. Commander Karaschelki stood stern faced and bewildered looking at the bodies.

"What's going on, sir?" Rominev asked, trying to look suitably shocked.

They came upon Makelov's body. Karaschelki did the sign of the cross over his dead comrade. After a moment's reverence, he turned to Rominev. "What do you think happened here, Rominev?"

"I don't know, sir." Rominev, wearing crime scene gloves, studied Makelov's body. "What was he doing here amongst this carnage?"

Karaschelki looked around at the mayhem, "Whatever it was, it got him killed."

"There was a shooting here last month, rival biker gangs were involved," Rominev stated.

Karaschelki's face reddened with anger as he studied the corpses. "I want anybody connected with this place brought in. You hassle all the biker gangs until they give you something, is that clear, Rominev?"

"Very clear, sir."

"I want you personally to check everything Makelov has been investigating. I want to know why he was in this bar."

"I'll find out. I promise, sir." And he would, Rominev decided, but he might not find what his colleagues wanted. Rominev would find what he wanted to find, and what he found would embroil Makelov in all this mess and make it obvious that Makelov was a cop on the take.

Chapter 24

Alexandria docks were noisy and bustling. That was what customs officer, Ali Shadiff, liked about the place. Whatever faults Alexandria had, it was never boring. He looked at the containers' rusting metal and flecking paint glimmering in the sun on the quayside. He ticked off each container on his sheet, paying particular attention to the yellow container with, *FARMING IMPLEMENTS* stencilled on the side. Hassan had paid him well to leave that container alone. Shadiff moved off along the quay, ignoring the activity by Hassan's men around the *FARMING IMPLEMENTS* container.

They were loading something on a lorry. The lorry moved quickly and the yellow container was loaded back on the freighter. Shadiff didn't want to know what had been taken out the container. He was just relieved when the lorry left the docks and was outside his jurisdiction. Outside the gates, Hassan watched from his Renault as the lorry thundered out of the docks. Hassan quickly followed as the lorry headed east along the coast road between Alexandria and Rashid.

Hassan kept close behind the lorry for a few miles, pulled alongside it, and signalled for the lorry driver to follow him. He led the lorry along a rutted road leading to an abandoned army camp. In a crumbling concrete garage inside the camp, the lorry pulled to a halt. Hassan walked over to the lorry. The driver got out of the cab. Hassan handed him an envelope full of money with an order: "Go for a walk, come back in a half-hour."

The driver wandered off. Hassan's men set to work, unloading the canisters from the container into the back of a waiting van. Hassan stood observing every step of the operation. Each canister was deadly, lethal to anybody who came in contact with the contents. After twenty minutes, the operation was complete. Hassan was satisfied. The lorry driver returned and went back to his cab. Shortly after, the lorry departed. Hassan checked they'd left no evidence of their presence at the camp and then followed the van out.

Hassan had earned every penny of the $250,000 that Mullah Omah was paying him for his services. When the van was safely on its way, Hassan stopped at a layby to call Omah.

He thought about the long cruise that awaited him. He'd be departing shortly. One thing was certain, when Omah unleashed the deadly genocide from the canisters on Egypt, Hassan would make sure he wasn't around.

Chapter 25

DI Wright called DCI Rowland over to his desk. DI Wright was working on his computer. "Moscow says the dental records and fingerprints are a match to a man called Valentino Ilyich. Ilyich is a former member of a Spetsnaz battalion. He was based near Moscow from 1998 to 2005."

"That sounds like our assassin," Rowland said.

"His record says he left the army by mutual consent in 2005. The Russian army say they know nothing about his life after this." Wright looked up from the screen.

"Well, we know something about what he's been up to," Rowland remarked, reading the printed resume. "We know that he's been involved with the Russian mafia as an assassin. We know he murdered Winterburn and his people, then murdered James Pike in Marseille."

"Pike was only twenty-one years old, sir."

"Sarah Appleton is blameless. She had no choice but to flee with her father, Detective."

"Maybe, sir." Wright paused. "I have to ask myself, when she asked Pike to go to Marseille, she must've realized she was putting his life in danger."

"It's young love, Inspector, young love is never sensible." Rowland looked at the print out. "Looking at the

Russian mafia link to the London killings, we have a massive opportunity here, Wright. Appleton was dealing with them for Winterburn, knows a lot about them."

"You want to make a deal with him, sir."

"I don't think we've got a choice, Wright. The information Appleton can give us about the Russian mafia's workings would be invaluable."

"Ilyich has been linked to several murders in Russia. The Russian police reckon he might be a mafia enforcer nicknamed 'Cobra.'" Wright read the information from the screen. "If Ilyich went to France to kill Appleton, then somebody must have been waiting for him to call them to confirm his success."

"We make a deal, then we need to talk with Organized Crime, find out what's relevant, what's worth dealing for." Rowland was already on the phone, dialling Organized Crime. If they were going to move, they had to move quickly.

Chapter 26

Appleton felt smug when they went to talk to him in the interview room. The fact that DCI Rowland was there with his sidekick—another cop Appleton didn't know—meant they'd come to talk.

They wanted to know the Russian mafia's inner workings and had decided Appleton was the man to teach them.

"So you're ready to talk about a deal," Carlton-Price said.

"You're in no position to make demands," Rowland said. "Superintendent Parker from Organized Crime will decide if what you've got is worth making a deal for."

"With what I can give you, there's a chance of closing down all sorts of financial links to organized crime. You might even bag a few of their leading lights in the process." Appleton laughed. "Please, don't tell me you want to give up all that to get me for stealing bonds from Winterburn."

"You stole tainted money from organized crime. You were working for mobster Winterburn, your daughter's boyfriend was murdered because of your involvement with these people," Parker stated coldly.

"Okay, I admit I've made mistakes—"

"Pike dead, a trail of mayhem. Yes, you could say you've made mistakes," Rowland said.

"My client is here to make a deal," Carlton-Price said. "We've discussed it. My client will tell you everything he knows about the Russians and Winterburn's operations. For full cooperation and financial details, he wants a pardon for both him and his daughter."

"You're asking a lot," Parker said. "How do we know what you've got is worth such a deal?"

Carlton-Price put his briefcase on the table. He unlocked it and took out a floppy disk. He handed the disk to Parker.

"On that disk are details of a Russian mafia account that they use to launder money through Jersey," Appleton stated. "I give you this as a gesture of faith. Take this away and look at it. If you're pleased, then we'll make a deal for the more detailed stuff."

Parker nodded. They'd check it out. The look on Appleton's face told Parker everything. Appleton knew he held aces in this deck, and Parker had already decided, if the Jersey account panned out, then this was a deal that Organized Crime couldn't afford to pass up.

Chapter 27

Mullah Omah sat staring at the flickering flames of the orange-red fire. Hassan was seated near-by, drinking coffee. Omah ran his fingers through his salt and pepper beard in a moment's reflection. "The infidels are among us, Hassan," he warned. "We can no longer just sit back and hope that the natural order of things will right itself and God will set up an Islamic Utopia."

Hassan feigned interest but never really listened. The Islamic extremists were full of bluster and their own importance. Hassan had found, apart from Nine/Eleven, their deeds rarely matched their words. "God is great!" he exclaimed.

"God has spoken to me, Hassan. God wants me to be the instrument that molds a new beginning for Arabs in this region."

Hassan bent forward in a few minutes of quiet prayer. He feigned a strong belief in Islam for the benefit of his Islamic backers. Reality meant that he was indifferent to all religions. When he knelt and prayed, he was praying to the only true religion he knew and understood—money. "The goods are ready for collection, Mullah Omah."

Omah smiled, snapped his fingers. A servant brought a bag full of money and handed it to Hassan. "That is the final payment for your part in the smuggling operation," Omah stated.

Hassan didn't count it. He'd found in some matters, like paying for services, men like Omah were men of honor. "Our business is concluded," Hassan said and stood.

"My men will go with you to collect the goods."

Hassan nodded respectfully and then left. He wanted to be holding the dangerous canisters for as brief a period as possible. He would take the men straight to the canisters. They were stored in an air-conditioned house on the outskirts of Cairo.

As they drove toward Cairo, Hassan noticed the Land Rover was sticking close behind his Shogun. Two hours later, they arrived at a terracotta-clad villa that gave a panoramic view of the smog-laden city. The canisters were quickly removed. Omah's men were not people to stand on ceremony.

After they'd left, Hassan checked the rented villa one last time. He picked up the brochure off the coffee table. The cruise he was embarking upon was setting sail from Cairo tomorrow, and the thought of the bio-weapons in Omah's hands made him decide the sailing time couldn't come quickly enough.

One thing he'd learned in all his dealings with them was that they were definitely mad enough to use them.

Chapter 28

Commander Debbie Thrower—head of Organized Crime—sat in her office. It was bland and functional. Thrower wasn't nicknamed the "Ice Queen" by her colleagues for nothing.

Parker sat in the offered chair and then told her what he had. "The trail leads back to a Russian called Vladimir Chernekov. After hours of working with Appleton, analysing the data he's given us, I'm convinced that Chernekov is one of the top Russian mafia leaders."

He was convinced that Appleton had no reason to lie with his freedom at stake.

"Be careful, Parker. Corruption in the Russian Police is rife. We don't want what we know getting back to this Chernekov."

"I've no intention of trying to close this Chernekov down. If we leave him operating, we can monitor his activities, pick up more on them, ma'am."

"You're the man in the field, Parker, it's your call."

What she meant was, if it went wrong, it was Parker's call and he'd take the blame.

"You won't regret it, ma'am." But as he left the room to carry on with his work, he had a feeling that *he* might.

Thrower picked up the phone on the desk. She called Middlemarsh at MI6. If you had a foreign problem, Middlemarsh was the man to talk to. "We have a problem in Russia," she told him. "You know what the situation is like there, the state of corruption. Nobody can be relied upon. We need to get inside Russia outside of official sources."

"So you called me."

"Your people seem to have a talent for such things. They're able to go places that mine can't."

"As complimentary as ever, Thrower."

"You're an expert at avoiding a damaging situation. You won't go bulldozing in." Thrower said. She knew how to flatter him, and Middlemarsh had an ego.

"I'll see what I can do," Middlemarsh said.

And, with that statement, Thrower knew that what she asked was as good as done.

Chapter 29

When the canisters were unloaded from the Land Rover, Mullah Omah watched in silence from his tent door. They hid the canisters quickly in a tent to be examined by Alijhad, a scientist from Cairo University. Omah watched Alijhad enter the canister tent and followed him inside.

"You shouldn't be in here," Alijhad warned. He was wearing protective clothing. Omah wore none. Alijhad pointed to his mask. "If there was a canister leak, it would kill you."

"I'm doing Allah's work. Allah will protect me until the task is done."

Alijhad didn't argue. Omah was their leader before God. Alijhad wouldn't dare question Omah's wisdom. "Would you please stand over there, master?" Alijhad asked.

Omah moved where directed in order to give Alijhad room. Alijhad unwrapped the canisters and laid them on a blanket. Each canister had *Bacillus Anthracis* stencilled on the front of them. The spores inside the canister would cause havoc if sprayed throughout a city.

Omah fought the urge to pace. "Can they be moved yet?"

"They need to be on the refrigerated lorry," Alijhad ordered.

Omah commanded his men to do what the scientist ordered. He hated science but, at the moment, it was something he needed to use to complete God's work. When he was Ayatollah of Egypt, he would wage war against those that preached it.

Alijhad supervised the loading. When the canisters were loaded and sealed inside the back of a refrigerated meat lorry, Alijhad nodded. "These containers need to remain frozen until they're ready for use."

"My men will do as you request." Omah hadn't come this far to fail through stupidity.

"If I knew what the targets were, I could advise you how best to deploy them."

"Such matters don't concern you," Omah barked. "You have been put on this earth to serve God in whatever way your skills allow."

"I'm sorry, Mullah Omah. I need to expunge the Western education from me through prayer."

Omah sighed. "The infidels have left a mark on all of us, Alijhad. This is why I need to take action. This is why, in Egypt, we need to reverse things. I want you to stay with the canisters until they are ready to be fitted to the planes." Omah engaged Alijhad with a fiery penetrating stare. "God's work must take precedence over everything else in your life."

"Allah be blessed!" Alijhad shouted.

Omah could see in the belief in the man's eyes and understood that he had nothing to fear from this disciple.

Omah went back to his tent. The glory hour was nearly upon them, and the infidel's Godless reign was nearly over.

Chapter 30

MI6 Agent Sean Rutter spoke Russian like a native. He'd learned at an early age that he had a penchant for languages, something MI6 had been quick to use when he'd joined them after leaving the SAS in 2003. They wanted him to look at a guy named Chernekov. Chernekov resided in the dachas owned by the rich and famous a few miles outside of Moscow.

Everything looked the same. Stalin Baroque, with its disfiguring effects, infested the place. The Communists had liked to make grandiose architectural statements, the streets designed as immense wide spaces for Red Army parades. Rutter drove past the Kremlin Towers and followed the highway out of the city.

He'd researched everything he could find on Chernekov. There wasn't much. His identity was immersed in layers of subterfuge. The subterfuge alone told Rutter that Chernekov was up to no good. He drove into the tree-lined suburbs, where the super-rich houses of the Moscow elite nestled. He passed several imposing walls and fences. All the houses were like fortresses, designed to keep people out. At the razor-wire-topped wall surrounding Chernekov's dacha, Rutter pulled to a halt. He noticed CCTV cameras at strategic points, didn't rate the system. A good surveillance system should always remain hidden.

He drove off and parked in a secluded backwater away from the surveillance cameras. He could hear barking guard dogs, another obstacle in the way of him penetrating the dacha's defences. He opened the boot and took out binoculars and other surveillance equipment, then skirted through the trees to the border of Chernekov's estate.

From the branches of a pine tree, he carefully studied the dacha. He noted the house's main drive had an expensive Mercedes parked by the door. He saw Alsatians roaming freely among the grounds. He set up a zoom-lens camera and prepared to take photos of anybody who entered or left the house.

Cold, drizzly rain soaked him. Aching with cramps, he prepared for his long vigil. The movie world of martinis and beautiful models was not for the real-life field agent. He removed a mint from his pocket and sucked it, one of the many that he would consume to alleviate the boredom throughout the day.

Chapter 31

Rominev had been tasked with the job of going through Makelov's things to find out what he was working on, discover why he'd been at Savian's bar. Through necessity, Rominev had become a good actor. As his colleagues looked on, Rominev meticulously went through Makelov's things. Apart from some dodgy porn mags buried beneath some papers, there was nothing of interest, a fact he reported to Karaschelki when he'd finished. Karaschelki sat back in his high-backed leather chair and couldn't mask his disappointment.

"So we still have no idea what he was doing there," Karaschelki said.

"I'm afraid not. Apart from finding he had a liking for Swedish porn, I found nothing, sir."

"Lose those magazines, Sergeant," Karaschelki ordered, briefly glancing at them. "I don't want his widow receiving these in his list of possessions."

"They're as good as lost, sir."

"I want you to keep pushing the biker gangs until something turns up," Karaschelki ordered. "The press claim, in light of recent incidents, that we've got a biker gang war on our hands. They're demanding we do something."

"We're doing all we can, sir. A cop was involved. All the men are willing to put extra time in to solve it."

"I need someone for this fast, Sergeant," Karaschelki said. "Make the bikers' lives a misery until they squeal."

"If we target their drug dealing operations, something will give, sir."

Rominev left Karaschelki to continue with the investigation. He wondered how long until some bright spark found a connection between Rominev and Makelov. It was almost time for Rominev to leave Moscow for good. First, he had to take care of some problems.

He headed to Chernekov's dacha. He had a final payment to collect for Karishen. He was to meet Karishen with the money at a truckers' café half way between Moscow and St. Petersburg. When Chernekov paid Rominev for the work he'd done, then Rominev was going to flee.

He stopped his car outside the doors of Chernekov's snow-encrusted dacha and waited for the dog handler to appear to usher him safely inside.

By the time he was inside, Rutter had taken his picture. It would go alongside the others in Rutter's rapidly growing dossier. All the people he'd taken photos of would be investigated, looking for links to organized crime. Rutter was pleased with his surveillance work to date. He took out two mints and sucked on them simultaneously in way of celebration.

Chapter 32

At Cairo airport, the security officers greeted Fasal with the usual stringent measures that the increase in terrorist activity in recent years had forced upon the authorities. Fasal stayed calm as he slowly made his way through customs. There was nothing officially to link him to terrorism, a fact verified by his straightforward passage through the security points.

The taxi driver gave Fasal a contemptuous glare, as he realized that Fasal was a local and he should know the going rate for the journey. As they nudged through the dense traffic Fasal thought of the poor unsuspecting souls trying to eke out a living. If only they knew how insignificant their pathetic worries were, since soon most of them would be dead.

In Islamic Cairo he alighted. He followed some back alleys away from the mosques, moving slowly through clammy dwellings, until he came to the dusty tight stairway leading to the flat he rented.

At his front door, he was greeted by his neighbor, Barak, standing nearby on the balcony, smoking.

"Has Allah been good to you, Barak?" Fasal asked.

"One of my daughters wants to marry a Libyan," Barak grumbled. "He runs a stall at the Khan el-Khalili souk. A Libyan. I ask you, Fasal, can any good come of it?"

Fasal patted Barak on the shoulder. "Who knows the minds of the young?"

Fasal unlocked his front door and entered his home. His flat was hot and sweaty. He opened windows but the heat was still unbearable. He looked through some letters on his doormat. A letter with an Alexandria postmark immediately caught his attention. The letter told him that the table the furniture restorer was repairing for him would be ready for collection on the seventh of November.

Omah sent everything in code. The translation of this code told Fasal that Omah wanted to meet him at the Alexandria safe house on the seventh November. Four days' time. Four days to get his report finished. Omah would expect it finished. Omah was not a man who tolerated anything other than complete professionalism from those around him.

Fasal had been in England, using the flight-trainer facility. Fasal's team had practised simulated runs over Cairo, Alexandria, and Port Said. These areas were where Omah intended to spray the canisters. Omah judged that the area of contamination would kill thousands, infect millions with the *Bacillus Anthracis* germ fallout.

The government wouldn't be able to cope with the fallout. The country would turn to anarchy. It would leave a vacuum. A vacuum that Omah and his followers would be ready to fill. The Islamic revolution would engulf Egypt, Omah's followers would blame the biological attack on the Jews.

The weather needed to be perfect. There was no room for error. They only had one chance for the attack. Fasal grew excited at Omah's call to arms. This was the moment in Fasal's life where he had the opportunity to serve God, and one thing was certain, Fasal intended to serve God well.

Chapter 33

The highway was cold and bleak, as only a Russian highway could be on a freezing autumn night. Rutter kept his tail car two cars distant. He had followed the policeman since he left Chernekov's dacha. The cop had gone to a Moscow Police station for an hour, then he'd left Moscow and headed out on the highway.

The cop was heading towards St Petersburg. He barely got halfway and turned off at a truckers' café. At the café, he parked and entered. Rutter parked his car behind a lorry, out of sight of the steamed-up café windows. In the dingy café lights, Rutter could see the cop sitting at a table talking to another man.

Rutter wanted to go inside, but decided that, in the tight café confines, he couldn't do it without being noticed. He decided to wait in the shadows, observing the meeting through the window. He didn't have to wait long. The meeting came to a quick conclusion. The man the policeman met left the café and got in a Saab parked in the corner.

Rutter rushed to his car and followed the Saab.

The Saab headed for St Petersburg. In the St Petersburg suburbs, Rutter closed the distance, followed the Saab around icy streets until it pulled to a halt in front of a house. Rutter parked his car and watched the man enter the house. He waited for a while and watched upstairs lights being turned on. When he was sure the man wasn't going anywhere, he noted the house number and street and left.

He rang London from a payphone, told them what he had. They ordered him to go to a hotel and stick with the Saab driver. London would check out the cop. Rutter went straight to a hotel and slept in a warm bed. The layers of deceit were starting to unfold in front of him. Now they had a connection between a Moscow cop and Chernekov. Chernekov's days were numbered.

Chapter 34

Fasal stood on the balcony of the apartment block that housed the safe house. He stared at the unhindered view of the murky polluted waters of Alexandria Harbor and decided the filthy water was a good analogy of the Egypt of today. He paused outside the apartment a moment then knocked.

Omah's bodyguard, Dravagi, answered. "Inside, quickly," he ordered.

Fasal entered. Dravagi shut and locked the door. They walked along the corridor to the living room, where they found Omah kneeling in prayer on a prayer mat. Fasal took his shoes off and stood in the corner, waiting in due reverence for Omah to finish praying.

At last, Omah finished and signalled for Fasal to sit opposite. "Did things go well in England, Fasal?"

"The pilots are ready to do God's bidding, Mullah Omah."

Omah smiled. "The hour of destiny has almost arrived. Within weeks, we will be ready. There are things that need to be taken care of in Israel, links that have to be established if we are to fool the world."

"Let Allah's will be done," Fasal said.

"It will be, Fasal. You will be told everything you

need to know when you need to know it," Omah stated. "They will be given adequate time to prepare."

"What happens after?" Fasal asked.

"Your pilots will be taken care of. We have plans for after." Omah was calm and confident. "You will be contacted in three weeks."

"Let Allah's will be done!" Fasal proclaimed.

Dravagi motioned Fasal out the room. The interview was over. Fasal left the apartment block via back alleys. He waited on the crowded train platform for the Cairo train, wondering about the people around him. Who would die, and who would survive the attack? He decided such questions were an irrelevance. If it was God's will, you survived. If not, you died. It was as simple as that.

Chapter 35

Rutter sat in his Moscow hotel room. He received a text on his mobile from MI6 analyst, Penelope Wainright. She told him about Boris Karishen, the man he'd followed, how Karishen was high up in the St Petersburg port authority. It made things interesting, Chernekov had sent the cop Rominev to meet this Karishen. The complex web was starting to unfold. If Chernekov was using Karishen, then he had to be smuggling something through St Petersburg. Wainright told Rutter she would put an agent on Karishen and that he should just concern himself with the Moscow side of the operation.

Rominev's apartment block was as bland and uninspiring as all the others were. The pathetic-looking silver birches, dotted between the buildings in austere plant beds, failed to break the relentless monotony. Rominev's old BMW was parked under a streetlight at the front of the building, meaning he was at home.

Rutter sat it out, parked in the shadows. An hour later, Rominev left his apartment and drove off. As Rominev's car disappeared from view, Rutter hurried across the street and up the stairwell. On the second floor, he arrived at Rominev's balcony. When he was sure the coast was clear, he rushed to Rominev's apartment, took out his skeleton keys, and opened the door. Wainright said that Rominev lived alone, but Wainright had been known to be wrong.

Rutter shut the door and stood silent and still, listening. Years as an agent had made Rutter alert to sound and movement. On certain occasions that alertness meant the difference between life and death. Under torchlight, Rutter methodically searched the apartment. Unsurprisingly, Rominev kept nothing incriminating there.

He heard a sound, turned his torch off. Someone was coming in the front door. Rutter couldn't get out the front door. He looked at the windows, but they were all locked. He had no time to do anything and had to improvise quickly. He darted into the bedroom and hid in Rominev's wardrobe. He left the wardrobe door slightly ajar so he could see who the intruder was. He took his silenced Beretta from his pocket and held it nervously.

A torch beam was darting along the passageway telling him this definitely wasn't Rominev. As the man entered the bedroom, Rutter could see the glow of the man's face in the torchlight. Rutter didn't know him. The only thing he knew for certain, the man wasn't Rominev.

Chapter 36

There was an angry mob of Arabs demonstrating by the settlement gates. They were trying to stop Jewish settlers from entering the settlement. Leon Stopowitz slowed his Land Rover to a crawl as he drove past them. The army unit that was guarding the settlement gates lifted the barrier and let Stopowitz enter.

If Stopowitz had his way, he'd have speeded up and run the Arab scum down. Their leader was shouting something through a megaphone. Stopowitz stuck two fingers up at him and then drove on. He pulled to a halt in the compound and was greeted by some of his followers carrying Galil assault rifles.

His stern-faced building manager, Cohen, greeted him.

"Is the building work on schedule?" Stopowitz asked.

"We're ahead of schedule. I've told the men to work harder," Cohen answered.

"We must push on. We need to finish the settlement earlier than we anticipated," Stopowitz stated, his voice cold.

"The men understand the need for speed," Cohen said.

Cohen opened the boot and removed the box of supplies. He took them into Stopowitz's house.

In the kitchen, Stopowitz's wife, Dinah, appeared. Her sultry eyes stared at her husband. "I wish you'd let others go for the supplies, Leon."

"As leader of this community, I must be prepared to do more of the dangerous tasks than the others." Stopowitz held his wife a moment. "I have to be inspirational to this community, my love."

"Being inspirational doesn't mean you need to get killed," Dinah argued.

Stopowitz sighed. "Until the settlement is established, I have to be at the forefront of everything. I need to show our followers I'm worthy of being their leader. I cannot do God's work in any other way."

Stopowitz left his wife to put the shopping away and went to the lounge to talk to Cohen. Cohen was seated, looking nervous and apprehensive. "There was an attack on the outer perimeter last night, a petrol bomb was thrown over the wall, and the guard put it out with a fire extinguisher."

"We need to build the fences higher and stronger, farther out, make sure they don't get the opportunity to get that close again, Cohen."

"We can't afford new defenses. We're already over budget for the defenses we've got."

"Then we'll have to go over budget to make sure this settlement is secure."

"And where do we get the money from?" Cohen grilled. "We're already overextended at the bank. They won't lend us any more money."

"I'll go and see them, ask for another loan."

Cohen decided he'd have to go with Stopowitz. Stopowitz was too blunt to deal with financial people. Because Stopowitz was a hard-liner, he couldn't understand why other people didn't share his vision.

"Ring them and arrange a meeting, Cohen."

Cohen departed to do Stopowitz's bidding. Stopowitz stepped out on the balcony and studied the brown scrub grass on the side of the hill the settlement was perched on. He pictured two rows of razor wire going back a hundred yards. He saw floodlights illuminating the gap between the wires making a close-quarter attack impossible.

Getting the funds to allow such a project to become a reality was his top priority. Stopowitz could see a not-too-distant future where the West Bank was flooded with Jewish settlements, and, as all his followers knew, each new build was a step nearer to total domination of the Holy Land by the Jews.

Chapter 37

The man didn't linger long in the bedroom. Rutter had his silenced Beretta out as he stepped from the wardrobe and followed the man along the passage. In the glare of torchlight, he could see the intruder was planting a bomb underneath a sofa.

Rutter switched the living room light on. "Put your hands up!"

The intruder was wearing a ski mask. He stared at the pistol Rutter had pointed at him, concluded he didn't have any options. The intruder slowly raised his hands above his head.

"Who are you?" Rutter asked. His question was greeted with silence. "If you don't tell me, I'm going to kill you."

The intruder smiled. "If I tell you who I am, then you'll kill me."

"If you tell me who you are and what you're doing here, I won't kill you."

"You saw what I was doing here. There's no way that I'm going to say anything. Your Russian has an American accent. What are you, an American spy?"

"I ask the questions," Rutter said. "I've caught you planting a bomb in a cop's house, attempting to murder a cop. They'll throw the book at you."

"A cop's house where a strange American is lurking. What will the police make of you, comrade?"

"Irrelevant. We both know this isn't going to the authorities. Just tell me who you are and what you're doing here, and I'll let you live."

The intruder smiled. "There's as much chance of you letting me live as Dynamo Moscow have of winning the Champions League next season."

"A few shots in the right places, I could make your death a slow one. If you don't cooperate, you could die in torturous agony." Rutter came close behind the man, expertly frisked him. He removed a Makarov pistol from a shoulder holster, a wallet with some personal details.

"If you're going to kill me, get on with it. Whatever you're going to do, I'm not talking."

Rutter stepped back a few paces and looked through the wallet. The intruder's name was Sergie Nikolov. Whether it was his real name or not was impossible to know until London checked it out.

"I'll be straight with you," Nikolov said, "I came here to kill the cop, Rominev, the bastard put my brother in prison."

"Bollocks!" Rutter countered. He knew a professional hitman when he saw one. "Disarm the bomb and pick it up."

Nikolov slowly did as Rutter requested. Nikolov hadn't had time to prime it before Rutter was upon him. Rutter decided Rominev could return at any moment, and it was time to get out of here. He ushered Nikolov outside. He kept the Beretta hidden beneath his jacket. They arrived at Rutter's car. Rutter unlocked the boot, told Nikolov to get inside it.

Nikolov hesitated.

"Look me in the eye, Comrade, Rutter said. Look me in the eye and decide if you think I'll kill you if you don't obey my instructions."

Nikolov made his decision and stepped into the boot. Rutter shut and locked it. He drove down by the river, stopped at a quiet spot, and threw the bomb into the dark swirling water. On his mobile, he rang Compton, the intelligence head at the embassy. Using the code for the meeting place, he arranged to meet Compton there.

Rutter drove across the icy Moskavitch Bridge and met Compton in the old merchants' quarter. Compton looked far from pleased to see him. "This is a fucking mess, Rutter!"

"I had no choice. I couldn't let him plant the bomb and kill Rominev."

"So, instead, you kidnapped the bomber and gave us a major headache."

Rutter didn't argue. The whole bloody business was a mess. If Nikolov was working for Chernekov, then his failure to kill Rominev would alert Chernekov to the fact that something was wrong. Whatever it did, as Rutter swapped cars and Compton's tail lights disappeared into the night, any secrets Nikolov had, Compton was just the man to get them out of him.

Chapter 38

Compton sat opposite Rutter in one of the bland safe house rooms. "You should have checked with us first before kidnapping Nikolov," he said.

"There wasn't time. I had to make an agent-in-the-field decision."

"London's fuming."

"If I'd left the bomb, he'd have blown up Rominev and killed most of his neighbors."

"Maybe it would have been easier to let Nikolov succeed."

"You can't mean that. Killing a load of innocents? We're meant to be on the side of truth and justice," Rutter said.

Compton leaned forward in his chair. "I've interrogated Nikolov personally. It appears he's a professional assassin hired by Chernekov to kill Rominev."

"I could've told you that."

"When Rominev isn't assassinated, Chernekov is going to realize something is wrong."

The phone rang in the other room. Compton left the room to answer it. Rutter took his Beretta out of his shoulder holster and checked it over. Compton came back into the room and noted Rutter checking over his Beretta.

"Do I need to take care of Nikolov?" Rutter asked.

"Put the gun away. Murder isn't the answer to everything, Rutter."

Rutter put his gun back in its holster. "So what are we going to do with him?"

"We're going to do nothing. London has made a deal with the Russians. I've been told to hand everything over to them," Compton said. "I've got to meet Colonel Dravisky of the FSB, in the foyer of the Intercontinental Hotel in an hour."

"And what do we get for doing their job for them?" an irritated Rutter asked.

"In the new spirit of Anglo-Russian cooperation, they'll owe us a favor."

"So we give them Nikolov."

"That's what London wants. I've got to arrange the hand over with Dravisky. You're to stay with Nikolov until I call you."

Rutter threw his hands up in frustration. "Double dealing and backstabbing, welcome to the world of democracy, Russia."

Compton left. Rutter sat thinking over events and didn't like any of it. He'd had dealings with the FSB before. Most of them were ex-KGB. Rutter had spent days accumulating information, all of it for nothing? He sat and shook his head.

He had to admit he sometimes hadn't a clue what he was fighting for anymore.

Chapter 39

Mullah Omah's agents Karuf and Rimidi met in Karuf's Jerusalem flat. Karuf looked out the dusty windows at the people wandering by in the street. He was obsessed with the specter of Mossad agents. "I've been keeping tabs on Stopowitz for over a month. Once a week, he drives to Jerusalem to take care of the commune's business. It's during that journey, he's at his most vulnerable."

Rimidi smiled, deciding it was all coming together. "Then that's when we take him."

"I'll set it up for the end of the week. On his next trip to Jerusalem, we take him."

"I'll relay your message to Mullah Omah," Rimidi said.

"Take a look at the forged documents."

Karuf took the documents out of the folder and laid them on the table. Rimidi studied them. He couldn't see a fault with any of them. They were perfect forgeries. The first was a customs shipment note from St Petersburg to Haifa for Russian farm machinery.

The second was a shipment order for *Bacillus Anthracis*, from the former Soviet Union's top-secret biological weapons center at Stepnergorsk, to be delivered to a Russian research laboratory. These were the documents for the Jews' files. They had to be hidden well, so that only a thorough search would be capable of finding them.

Karuf lifted a case from under his seat and laid it on the table. Inside was the equipment for the operation. Small arms, handcuffs, incapacitating drugs, plus the Israeli Army uniforms they were going to wear when they set up the bogus checkpoint.

Karuf had no illusions. If captured, by wearing the army uniforms, the Jewish authorities were sure to give them the death penalty. They had false documents that said they were Jordanians, yet another wall of confusion to fool the infidels.

"Have we forgotten anything?" Rimidi was on only his second mission for Omah.

Karuf decided Rimidi had a lot to learn. Omah never made mistakes.

"I've checked everything, and what we need is there," Karuf said.

They put everything back into the case then under the table. The sun was slowly setting. They both prepared for prayer. In the distance, they could hear the mullah from the local mosque calling his flock to prayer. They both ignored the call. They would stay in Karuf's flat and pray quietly. It was too risky to announce their presence by going to public prayer. Karuf had already decided that Jewish spies had infiltrated Jerusalem's mosques and were noting everything.

After prayer, they would leave on their mission. Step one was to plant the Russian documents in Stopowitz's Jerusalem offices. God's work never stopped, Karuf thought, as he knelt on the prayer mat and began to pray.

Chapter 40

Chernekov sat in his study chair, contemplating recent events. He looked at the English Victorian grandfather clock in the corner of his study plodding its inexorable beat. It was just after midday. Nikolov was meant to ring him at midday confirming the kill. Chernekov called his trusted lieutenant, Kamustin, to his study.

When Kamustin was seated opposite, Chernekov sighed. "Nikolov hasn't called. I think he's failed."

"Nikolov never fails, boss."

"There's a first time for everything, Kamustin." Chernekov reflected momentarily. "I think it's wise to conclude that he's failed. I want security at the dacha stepped up immediately, then I want you and some of the boys to go and check on Rominev. If Rominev isn't dead, then kill him."

"Do you want it to look like an accident?"

"Just fucking kill him! The cocky arsehole is starting to become a real pain in the arse." Chernekov wondered if Rominev had caught Nikolov in the act of planting the bomb, if so, Chernekov needed to be worried.

"What about Nikolov?"

Kamustin wanted to get his mission clear and precise. Chernekov was not a man who tolerated failure from subordinates.

"Try to find Nikolov. If you can't find him, then your priority is to kill Rominev."

Kamustin nodded then left. Chernekov grabbed the malt whisky bottle from a nearby drinks cabinet and poured himself a glass of it. He needed to keep his nerve. Rominev was brutal. The slaughter in Savian's bar perpetrated by him had shown how ruthless he could be.

The phone on Chernekov's desk rang. It was his private line that few people knew the number for. Nikolov might have succeeded, Chernekov thought. He snatched up the phone. There was a pause on the other end of the line.

"It's, Rominev, we need to meet," Rominev said finally.

Chernekov sat in his chair, steadied himself. "Come to my dacha at three o'clock."

The answer Rominev now gave would tell Chernekov if the man knew of his treachery.

"I'll be there," Rominev said and then hung up.

Chernekov decided that Rominev didn't know about Nikolov. Chernekov rang Kamustin. "Get back here now. Rominev is coming to us."

"What about Nikolov?"

"Keep the boys looking. I want you back here."

Chernekov put the phone down and smiled to himself. Nikolov had obviously bungled, but Rominev didn't know about it. Chernekov opened his desk drawer and took out the La France silenced Colt .45 pistol that he kept there. He slipped it into his jacket pocket. When Rominev arrived, Chernekov would be ready to finish the job that Nikolov obviously couldn't.

Chapter 41

In the side street just off Red Square, Rutter stood waiting by the Volvo. FSB Agent Konstantin Zahrin watched the British agent from the shadows of a doorway. His commander, Colonel Dravisky, had considered having the British agent tailed. He'd decided against it. Dravisky had decided to cooperate with the British on this. They were forthcoming and obviously after future favors.

The first thing Rutter noticed about Zahrin was his size. Rutter was over six feet, but Zahrin dwarfed him. Zahrin showed him his FSB identification. They briefly shook hands. Rutter decided Zahrin's strength matched his size. He handed Zahrin the Volvo keys.

"He's in the boot," Rutter said. "I'd appreciate it if you took it back to the hire car company when you've finished with it."

"Count it done, comrade," Zahrin said.

Rutter walked off. Within moments, he was back in the bustle of Red Square. Zahrin had looked Rutter in the eye, could see Rutter was a professional and would be impossible to tail.

Zahrin drove the Volvo to a car park at the back of FSB headquarters. He opened the boot to find a handcuffed Nikolov huddled inside. In the old days of the KGB, Nikolov would have been dragged inside, and they'd have tortured the information out of him. Zahrin contented himself with just helping Nikolov out the car and leading him inside.

He sat Nikolov down in a chair in an interview room while a FSB guard stood by the door. Colonel Dravisky entered the room.

"I want to see my lawyer," Nikolov said.

"You're not in a position to bargain, Nikolov," Dravisky stated. "You were caught planting a bomb at a police officer's flat, I could have you tried and executed as a terrorist."

"I'm no terrorist," Nikolov said.

"You've already told our colleagues that you were sent by Chernekov to kill Sergeant Rominev of the Moscow police. That alone is enough to condemn you," Dravisky stated. "You're facing attempted murder charges. Your only chance of doing yourself a favor is by telling us everything you know about Chernekov."

"I don't know anything about Chernekov."

"Don't be stupid, Nikolov. We've got your taped conversation admitting that Chernekov was paying you to kill Rominev. The case against you is rock solid. Do yourself a favor. Tell us what you know about Chernekov and make a deal."

Nikolov sat with his arms folded. "That confession was obtained using drugs. None of that confession would stand up in a courtroom. I've got nothing more to say until my lawyer is present."

"It's your funeral," Dravisky grumbled, not bothering to get heavy-handed yet. When they interrogated Rominev and Chernekov, they'd piece everything together.

Dravisky ordered Zahrin to lock Nikolov in a cell

then ordered a group of officers to assemble in a briefing room.

Half-hour later, Dravisky stood in front of them. "As you can see, gentlemen, with Rominev's involvement in all of this, I want the police kept out of it. FSB is going to handle this, keeping a tight lid on everything."

Dravisky didn't trust the police. Rominev was corrupt. It made you wonder how many others in the Moscow division were on the take. One thing was certain, Dravisky didn't know who was on the take and who wasn't.

"Do we bring Chernekov and Rominev in, sir?" a fresh-faced agent at the front of the room asked.

"I want five men to find Rominev and bring him in, and I want an armed unit to raid Chernekov's dacha," Dravisky ordered.

His men hurried off to obey. Dravisky decided they didn't have time to arrange surveillance on Chernekov. They had to act fast, before Chernekov realized something was wrong, before Chernekov had a chance to flee.

Chapter 42

The drive to Jerusalem was long and dangerous. Stopowitz turned onto the slip road that led to the East Jerusalem road. The sun would be up in an hour, and the chill of the night would be replaced by the insufferable heat of the day.

To his side, Cohen sat, nervously staring at the briefcase. "Don't worry, Cohen," Stopowitz said, "I put everything in the briefcase before we left."

"It's important that we always keep our files in order. Our enemies in government are always looking for excuses to break open our files and see what we're involved in," Cohen warned.

"That's why I need you with me, Cohen. With you always nagging me at my side, how can I make a mistake and fail?" Stopowitz glanced at Cohen and could see he was irritated. "I was only joking, Cohen. You know that you're an invaluable member of the commune."

They drove in silence along the dusty road. Cohen kept his Browning pistol on his lap. Israel was not a place Cohen ever felt safe in these days. Until the West Bank was swarming with Jewish settlements and they totally dominated the Palestinians, it was always going to be that way.

He felt like a Wild West settler in Indian country, and it was playing hell with his nerves.

"Another bloody roadblock," Stopowitz moaned, seeing a barrier strewn across the road.

An army jeep was parked next to it, and a couple of soldiers guarded the barrier.

The soldiers waved them down. Stopowitz stopped at the barrier. The soldiers came around the side of the vehicle, one toward Stopowitz, the other toward Cohen. Torchlight shone in Cohen's face. It was hard for him to make out anything in the darkness. Suddenly, the door was opened, and Cohen felt the cold barrel of a Galil assault rifle digging into his ribs.

"Step slowly out the car and lay face down on the ground," Karuf ordered, grabbing the pistol off Cohen's lap.

Cohen slowly obeyed. As he lay helpless, Karuf handcuffed his hands behind his back. To his side Cohen could see Stopowitz was suffering a similar fate. Cohen felt a needle being jabbed in his buttock. As the drug entered his blood stream, his eyes became heavy, his consciousness faded.

When Karuf judged Cohen was unconscious, he carried him to the jeep and dumped him in the back. Rimidi dumped an unconscious Stopowitz next to Cohen, and then they hid them under a blanket. Rimidi took Stopowitz's Land Rover and drove off. Karuf quickly took down the roadblock barrier and dumped it in a nearby ditch they'd dug beforehand.

Once the barrier was buried, Karuf drove the jeep to a safe house in a village just outside of Hebron. Karuf hid the jeep in the house's garage. Rimidi arrived on a motorbike minus the Land Rover an hour later. They embraced each other.

"Allah, be praised," Karuf said.

"Allah, be blessed!" Rimidi said.

Karuf's ambush plan had worked. Omah's followers had long-established smuggling routes across the Sinai into Israel. They were now going to smuggle Stopowitz and Cohen to Egypt along such routes. Omah would be pleased. Omah would soon see that his faith in Karuf and Rimidi had been justified, Rimidi decided.

Chapter 43

Rominev parked behind a cluster of damp sodden trees about a mile short of Chernekov's dacha. When Rominev got home from work, he'd found things moved in his apartment. Someone had been in there. His colleagues had no inkling that he was working for Chernekov, so Rominev decided the only person with anything to gain by searching Rominev's apartment was Chernekov.

He'd been a fool to think that Chernekov would play it straight. It was time that Chernekov was made aware of the facts of life.

Rominev checked his pistol over then put it in his shoulder holster. He checked his ankle holster where he had a Chinese 7.62mm pistol Type 77 hidden. He glanced at his watch. It was just before three o'clock. He started his engine and got moving. He opened the window and let a cold blast of air waft over him. He wanted his senses to be alert when he reached the dacha.

He arrived at Chernekov's gates, and, after a brief surveillance camera check, was allowed access. Kamustin was waiting when he stepped out his car.

"It's feeding time. The dogs are in the kennels," Kamustin reassured him as they entered the house.

By the door, there were two guards, instead of one. At Chernekov's study door, another guard stood waiting. Kamustin knocked and entered. Rominev followed.

Chernekov was seated behind his desk. "I'm a busy man, Rominev. This had better be important."

"You sent someone to search my apartment."

Chernekov sighed. "I don't deny it. I have to be sure about the people who work for me."

"I've proved myself on many occasions to you. You've got no need to doubt me."

"The cemetery is full of people who showed too much trust in people, Rominev." Chernekov grabbed his pistol from beneath some paperwork and pointed it at Rominev. "You're a fool if you trusted me."

Rominev thought about going for his Beretta, but the realization that to his side Kamustin's pistol was also out made that impossible. Kamustin pressed his PSM firmly in Rominev's back, removed Rominev's Beretta, and slipped it into his own pocket. He searched Rominev's coat pockets, showed his inexperience by not checking Rominev's ankles.

"Do you really think I'd come here after discovering you don't trust me without taking precautions?" Rominev cautioned.

Chernekov laughed. "Dead men tell no tales."

"This dead man will," Rominev warned. "I've been carefully documenting our transactions over the years. This, plus all the information concerning your criminal activities, is in the hands of a friend. If my friend doesn't get a call from me with a specific code-word once a day, he's been instructed to hand over everything I've given him to the police."

"I think Sergeant Rominev has been reading too much Agatha Christie, Kamustin," Chernekov said. Kamustin laughed, even though he had no idea who this

Agatha Christie woman was. "A few hours in Kamustin's hands and you'll be in so much pain you'll be begging to be allowed to call your friend with the code-word."

"You don't know me very well—"

Kamustin punched Rominev in the back, causing him to stumble over a chair. Chernekov laughed. He wasn't laughing when Rominev fired the Type 77 into Kamustin's forehead, or when the second bullet hit Chernekov's gun arm ripping open muscle and tissue. Chernekov dropped his weapon and fell to the floor.

Rominev scampered over to Chernekov. He grabbed Chernekov by the throat and pulled him behind the desk. As he arrived there, the study door opened and the guard entered. Rominev held his pistol to Chernekov's head. "Tell your guard to step out the study and shut the door behind him." Chernekov hesitated. "Tell him or I'll blow your fucking brains out!" Rominev shouted.

Chernekov's spirit of self-preservation was strong. "He's got a gun on me, Tanin. Step outside the study and shut the door."

Tanin left the room.

"In a minute, we're going to see if your men really know how to obey orders, Chernekov."

Rominev would have to use Chernekov as a hostage to get to his car. It was a bloody mess. Nothing had gone how he'd planned since he'd arrived at the dacha.

"All my men will be up at the house, waiting for you, Rominev. In chess, it's called a stalemate."

Rominev shrugged. Whatever it was, he would shortly be going out of here with Chernekov. From here to his car was about a hundred meters. A hundred meters past armed guards. Rominev didn't know whether he could make it. Still, he had no other option but to try.

Chapter 44

Colonel Dravisky stood frozen in the icy trees, waiting for the last of his men to get into position. He wanted to be closely involved in the raid on Chernekov's dacha. Dravisky had been looking at Chernekov's file. He was a distasteful character linked to a string of criminal activities. He was suspected of being involved in fire bombing some Moscow restaurants set up by the old cooperative system back in the late 1980s. When some of the restaurants became successful, the mafia moved in asking for protection money. Those that refused to pay felt the mafia's wrath and had their restaurants torched.

A young Chernekov had been brought in for questioning over the fire bombings. He'd stood firm. The police had never been able to muster enough proof for a conviction. The harsh constraints put on the FSB by the new democratic institutions meant that pursuing Chernekov with uncompromising authority of the old days was no longer possible.

Zahrin came over to Dravisky. "Everyone is in position, sir."

"Let's go then," Dravisky ordered.

Zahrin conveyed the orders over his walkie-talkie.

The area was soon alive with agents moving on the dacha. A van with a battering ram on the front of it drove up to the main gate and smashed it down. Cars raced behind the van up the gravel drive to the house.

As the agents jumped out the cars, guard dogs ran at them. Rapid bursts of gunfire hit the snarling dogs. Within moments, the dogs were dead. There was gunfire coming from the house. The agents cautiously approached it, using whatever cover was available. A barrage of small arms fire erupted in the corridor as they broke down the front door.

FSB agents dropped dead and wounded around Zahrin, Zahrin dove for cover behind a sofa. He fired his Heckler and Koch P7 pistol in the gunfire's direction.

Wounded FSB agents lay moaning in the corridor. Pinging bullets ripped plaster above Zahrin. A sustained bout of gunfire from the FSB, and Chernekov's guards at the end of the corridor were dead. Zahrin, at the front of his men, paused outside the study doors. Zahrin reloaded. The dead guards had fought viciously to protect the study. That told Zahrin all he needed to know. If Chernekov was anywhere in the dacha, he was in that room. Zahrin decided there was only one way to find out for sure. Slowly he started to turn the study door handle.

Chapter 45

When Stopowitz awoke, his mouth was dry and his body was sweaty and dehydrated. The room he was in was dark. He looked around the room, trying to make out objects. His blurry eyes finally started to focus and adjust to his surroundings. He tried to move his hands, but couldn't. He was handcuffed to a radiator pipe.

He started to note the contents of the room. There was a stack of boxes in the corner. Up against a wall, he could see a chest of drawers. He listened for sounds. He could hear Arab voices in another room. He tried to remember what had happened to him. His memory was hazy and confused. He remembered Cohen lying on the ground nearby when they'd been taken at the army checkpoint. Whether Cohen was alive or dead was impossible to know, as Stopowitz hadn't seen Cohen since.

He pulled at the handcuffs. They didn't budge. They were too solidly attached to the radiator pipes. The door to his side suddenly opened and the room was bathed in light from the corridor.

A man entered the room carrying a water bottle and a rice cake. He put them down near Stopowitz. "Here's food and water."

Stopowitz guzzled down the water quickly, but was more restrained when he ate the rice cake. "Why have you kidnapped me?"

"No questions."

"I'm not a wealthy man," Stopowitz said.

"No questions, Jew." The man left the room a moment, returned with a child's potty. He placed it on the floor near Stopowitz. "This is your toilet." He started toward the door.

"Is my colleague alive?" Stopowitz asked.

"No questions," the man said then left.

When the door shut, the room was dark again. Stopowitz was left with his thoughts. He thought about his wife and children. Those hours of pretend fighting with his son, Malachi. Would he ever see his son again? If they wanted to murder him, then surely he'd already be dead.

If the Palestinians thought they could win by killing Stopowitz, they were wrong. There were always others out there willing to take up the mantle. The settlers would remain strong. The generations to come would thank Stopowitz and Cohen for the sacrifice they were about to make. In his mind, Stopwitz saw a grown-up Malachi looking at Stopowitz's grave with pride. He tried to retain that image in his head and decided that image would sustain him through what was to come.

Chapter 46

Rominev could hear gunfire in the corridor outside Chernekov's study. Whatever was happening, he decided it didn't bode well for his situation. He had to get out of the dacha, fast.

"We need to get out of here. If there's a way, tell me now," Rominev ordered Chernekov.

"If I tell you a way out, then as soon as we're clear of the dacha, you'll kill me. It doesn't sound much of a deal to me, does it, Rominev?"

"Whoever is out there attacking the dacha has come for you, Chernekov. If we don't get out of here, we're both going to die."

Chernekov smirked. "Well, at least you'll die with me."

"Get me out of here, and I'll let you live." Rominev was prepared to offer Chernekov anything.

There was a hectic gun battle raging outside the study. The attackers seemed to have a lot of firepower. It was only a matter of time before they overwhelmed Chernekov's men.

"How do I know I can trust you?" Chernekov asked.

"You don't." Rominev stared long and hard at Chernekov. "Listening to what's going on out there, you're no longer a threat to me, Chernekov. We get out of here, all you'll have on your mind is self-preservation. I'll be the least of your problems."

A loud burst of gunfire erupted in the corridor. It made Chernekov come to a decision. "I need to get some things from my safe."

"Get them," Rominev ordered. "Remember, I'll be right behind you looking at everything you do."

Chernekov removed some leather bound volumes off a bookcase, behind it was a wall safe. He put the combination in, started to open the safe door, Rominev prodded his gun harder in Chernekov's back. Blood from Chernekov's earlier wound began to drip on the carpet.

"Remember, I'm watching your every move," Rominev told Chernekov.

Chernekov fumbled bank books and bonds into a leather bag. When he'd put everything in the bag, he lifted another book off a shelf and pressed a button behind it.

A door opened, leading to a secret passage. "This tunnel goes for a few hundred yards and comes up in a garage. In the garage is an E-Series Mercedes I keep for emergencies."

They entered the tunnel, Chernekov pressed a button inside the door and the passage door shut behind them. Rominev kept close behind Chernekov as they went down some steps and then along a metal strutted passageway.

They reached a hatch above them. The hatch could be reached via a ladder attached to the wall.

"Above the hatch is the garage," Chernekov said. "You'll have to lift the hatch. With my wound, I can't lift it."

Chernekov was now at Rominev's mercy. Rominev climbed the ladder and opened the hatch. The garage was quiet. In the distance, Rominev could hear gunfire. He helped Chernekov up the ladder. "Where are the keys?" Rominev asked.

"In the drawer on the right."

Rominev found the keys and opened the garage door. "Get in!"

Chernekov got into the passenger seat. Rominev got into the driver's seat. He put his pistol to the right of the seat out of Chernekov's reach. The state Chernekov's arm was in, he was in no position to attempt to wrestle the gun from Rominev.

Rominev carefully edged the Mercedes forward. They slowly pulled out the garage, well away from the main house. He edged down the drive. There were vehicles near the house. Rominev put his foot to the floor—if they were going to get out of the dacha, it had to be now.

Chapter 47

The gunfire ended. The corridor in front of the study lapsed into a deathly silence. Zahrin was close behind his men when they arrived at the door. The guards had fought savagely to defend the study, which meant that Chernekov was inside the room.

Through the study door, Zahrin could hear the muffled sound of voices. The voices suddenly became silent. A battering ram was found and Zahrin's men broke the door down. The wood splintered. They funnelled inside but there was no gunfire from within. Zahrin's men quickly searched the room and found nobody alive just a dead Kamustin.

"There were voices. Someone was in here," Zahrin said. "Look for another exit."

"I've found something," an agent said moments later.

Behind the books the agent had found the button that opened the door to the escape passage. Zahrin pushed it and the door hidden in the wall opened. Inside the doorway was a trail of blood leading along a passage. Zahrin and his men hurried along the passage.

Ahead of them they could hear the clunking sound of feet on a ladder. Moments later, they arrived at the foot of the ladder. The blood trail ended here, indicating that

Chernekov had gone wherever the ladder went.

Above them, an engine strummed to life. Zahrin rushed up the ladder. As he slung open the hatch, a Mercedes sped out of the garage. Zahrin fired shots at the rear car window but the glass didn't shatter. Shots fired at the tires by his men had no effect either. Obviously, Polycarbonate glass and Kevlar rubber. The Mercedes was of the armored variety favored by Russia's elite.

"Damn!" Zahrin shouted.

There were no other cars in the garage, no chance of immediate pursuit. The car sped quickly out of view. Zahrin was quickly on the radio, barking orders for assistance. Zahrin could see the road led through the trees away from the dacha.

Chernekov had obviously planned his escape. A man with many enemies usually did.

Dravisky's car appeared. Zahrin hurriedly got in. Under Zahrin's directions, Dravisky sped after the Mercedes.

"The BMW that was parked at the front of the dacha is registered to Rominev," Dravisky said as he drove aggressively after them. He found it hard to mask his anger that Chernekov had escaped. "We had them both, and we let the bastards get away."

Zahrin decided the word "we" meant "you" in Dravisky's mind. Dravisky would lay the blame for this blunder squarely at Zahrin's feet. They drove on until they reached the Moscow outskirts, found no sign of the fleeing Mercedes. Two hours further search by all available units, and Dravisky came to the only possible conclusion, Chernekov and Rominev had managed to escape.

Chapter 48

This part of his job Inspector Max Slemen of the Israeli police hated. A policeman's lot in life was always to bring bad news to people. He sat in the offered chair at the Stopowitzs' apartment. "I'm sorry, Mrs. Stopowitz, we can find no sign of your husband or Mr. Cohen."

"Then the Palestinians must have him," Mrs. Stopowitz reluctantly concluded.

"I'd like a list of your husband's associates, any contacts you know about." Slemen was desperate for any information that might lead to something. So far, they had nothing, not even a sniff of a clue as to what fate had befallen Stopowitz and Cohen.

Mrs. Stopowitz fumbled in a drawer, took out her husband's address book. "This has everybody he knows in it."

"I'll have the names checked out," Slemen pocketed the book. "You said he was going to Jerusalem to take care of business?"

"Every Thursday, he always goes to Jerusalem to take care of the community's financial affairs. Leon is a creature of habit. He wouldn't miss these business meetings for anything."

Stopowitz had stuck to the same routine. Foolish man, Slemen thought. By sticking to the same routine, he'd left himself open to a terrorist attack. Stopwitz and Cohen had never arrived at the sect's Jerusalem offices.

"I've put out an APB on their Land Rover. I've circulated their photos to all police and army units. We're doing everything we can to find them, Mrs. Stopowitz."

"You're too late, Inspector, the Palestinian bastards have killed them."

"We don't know that, Mrs. Stopowitz."

Mrs. Stopowitz sighed. "Can you really put your hand on your heart and say that you think they're still alive?"

"Until I hear anything to the contrary, then I will assume that they're still alive. You have my promise that my men will do everything within our power to find them."

"The army should be out there, searching Palestinian houses in the West Bank. It's obvious who's taken them. They were the only ones who had reason to harm them."

Slemen decided an argument with Mrs. Stopowitz about Palestinians' rights was pointless. The extreme sect she belonged to thought of Palestinians as interlopers and expected the government to run roughshod over them.

"I'll have the route between your road and the Jerusalem road thoroughly searched," Slemen reassured her and then left.

Outside, seated in his car, he decided the most likely scenario was that the PLO had killed them and the Land Rover and their bodies would never be found. He slowly drove out the settlement and was greeted by the hostile glares of the settlers. The settlers would look upon anything other than the safe return of their men folk as police incompetence.

As he drove past an IDF checkpoint, his police vehicle received hateful stares from some Palestinians. Slemen smiled, decided his profession was the most hated in the country, and, as an Israeli policeman, you couldn't please any of the people any of the time.

Chapter 49

The Mercedes hurtled along tree-lined country roads. Rominev glanced across at Chernekov and decided that the loss of blood from his wound was making him very ill.

"Where are we going?" Chernekov asked.

"We can't go to Moscow. The police will concentrate their search there." Rominev had already decided that soon they'd be parting company. He had shot Chernekov and had a hand in destroying his crime empire—something a man full of bile and hatred like Chernekov was never likely to forget.

The sun was setting and the wintry green and gray colors, together with the brightness of the houses, were in stark contrast to Moscow's grime. Rominev decided the moment of decision had come.

"What happens when we stop?" Chernekov asked.

"We go our separate ways," Rominev stated. "I've no need to kill you, Chernekov. You've got enough problems, with the police after you and your gangland empire collapsing, to worry about revenge on me."

Rominev drove up to a small, secluded railway station. He parked the Mercedes next to a clapped-out Skoda and a rusting tractor. "I get out here."

Rominev trained his pistol on Chernekov, lifted Chernekov's bag off the back seat. He fumbled inside, taking just a couple of bundles of notes out of it. He put the bag back on the seat. He slipped his pistol inside his shoulder holster and stepped out the car. Rominev wanted Chernekov to take the car. The car was the vehicle the police would be trying to trace. The car made Rominev vulnerable.

Chernekov slipped into the driving seat and was quickly gone. As Rominev stepped on the cold desolate platform, the temperature was dropping quickly. He sat on a bench and thought about his escape bag full of money with new identity documents zipped up inside. The bag was waiting in a safety deposit box in a Moscow bank. It was two hours away by train. After he collected the bag, he'd be out of Moscow and disappear off the radar for good. As he wrapped his coat tighter around his cold body, he thought about all the things he'd miss about Russia. The one thing he wouldn't miss was the cold. No Russian ever missed the cold. If they said they did, they were lying, he decided, as the train slowly trundled to a halt in front of him, and he and his weary body boarded it.

Chapter 50

Karishen and his girlfriend Natasha sat in a Helsinki hotel restaurant, eating an expensive meal. A statuesque pianist in the corner rattled off melodies as they ate.

Natasha leaned across the table and lightly kissed Karishen. "Thank you for a lovely weekend."

Karishen poured some champagne into Natasha's almost empty glass. "You deserve it. You've got a lot to put up with, darling."

Natasha paused a moment, deep in thought. "Will you ever leave her?"

Karishen noticed that Natasha's eyes seemed to sparkle in the candlelight's glow. "I don't know. With the boys still at school, now isn't the time to leave her."

"What about when the boys have left school?" Natasha pressed him.

"Things will be different when they're grown up," Karishen promised.

Natasha wondered if Karishen would ever leave his wife. The fact that he was in Helsinki with Natasha showed that he didn't love his wife. "I want to be with you, Boris."

Natasha meant it. She knew men much better looking

than Karishen, but they were pigs compared to Karishen. He was a complete romantic and knew how to treat a woman.

"There'll be more weekends like this," he lied.

The truth was this trip to Helsinki was costing him a fortune. He'd almost used all the money up that Chernekov had paid him for getting the container through customs. When that money was gone, he had no other revenue available for luxury trips.

"Let's enjoy the moment," Natasha suggested. "We'll be going home tomorrow."

Karishen held her hand tightly across the table. The champagne bottle was empty. "Shall I order another one?"

"No, let's do something else."

Under the table, he could feel the soft touch of her silky stockings against his trousers. It meant she'd taken one of her stilettos off. Karishen found her to be at her most desirable when she was drunk and uninhibited. In his trousers, he could feel himself getting hard thinking about the prospect of sex. He quickly signed the chit for the meal and they hurried to their room.

In the foyer, FSB Special Agent Conan Varras pretended to read a newspaper and noted all this. The hotel was ridiculously expensive. It should have been way beyond what someone like Karishen could afford. Varras had followed many people for the FSB over the years. He knew the look that Karishen and his mistress had in their eyes when they left the restaurant. It was the look of sex, a look that meant they'd be occupied for the next few hours. He stepped outside the hotel, took out his mobile phone, and rang Colonel Dravisky.

"I've found, Karishen, sir. He's staying at the Northern Lights Hotel in Helsinki." It hadn't been difficult.

They'd bugged Karishen's home and office phones.

They'd also bugged his wife's sister's phone in Moscow. When Karishen called his wife at her sister's, they'd traced the call back to the Northern Lights Hotel in Helsinki.

"He's booked into a room with some young tart," Varras added.

"Stick with him until he's back on Russian soil," Dravisky ordered. "When he's back on Russian soil, we'll bring him in for interrogation."

Varras went back inside the hotel to continue his mission.

In Moscow, Dravisky's office phone rang moments after he'd finished talking to Varras. It was Zahrin in charge of looking through everything they'd found at Chernekov's dacha.

"I've found something. You'd better get up here, sir."

"I've got a meeting with Commander Mazinsky in an hour, Zahrin," Dravisky protested.

"Cancel it, sir, this is more important."

What could be more important than a meeting with Commander Mazinsky? Dravisky wondered. Whatever it was, Zahrin knew better than to break up such a meeting without good cause.

"I'm on my way," Dravisky stated and decided whatever it was, he had to know.

Chapter 51

Seated behind Chernekov's desk viewing documents, bespectacled Zahrin looked like a worried man. Dravisky, sitting opposite, looked equally worried.

Zahrin handed Dravisky the documents. "These are dispatch documents for a consignment of *Bacillus Anthracis* that was moved by the Director of Stepnogorsk Biological Weapons Center in Kazakhstan to a government research laboratory in Southern Russia in the 1990s," Zahrin stated.

Dravisky carefully studied the documents, muttering as he read. "And why would Chernekov have these documents at his dacha?"

"They were hidden in a secret panel behind some books, sir. Chernekov's dacha appears to house a lot of secrets."

"I want the place ripped apart," Dravisky ordered.

Zahrin had his men doing that already. To humor Dravisky, he said he'd do so.

"We've known for a long time that the mafia has penetrated the arms trade. I'm afraid this might be another worrying side line. Maybe the mafia are involved in trying to sell biological weapons to governments or terrorists," Dravisky warned.

"That's a horrific thought, sir."

"This situation has now become much more critical, Zahrin. We need to find out who they've sold the anthrax to. I want every man we can spare on this." Dravisky thought about the danger of these weapons.

If Chernekov was selling biological weapons, he'd have to import them from somewhere. Transportation, transportation was the key to the buyer.

Chernekov had been dealing with Karishen, with Rominev as an intermediary. It made bringing in Karishen for questioning even more important.

"It would explain why Rominev was meeting Karishen, sir."

"Without talking to Chernekov, we can't know how involved the mafia are." Dravisky looked at the consignment sheet and noted to which government research center in Southern Russia it was transferred to from Kazakhstan. He pointed at the laboratory address. "And what about this place?"

"The laboratory was shut down by the government eight years ago. The government decided that such establishments were a drain on resources, and they were phased out, sir."

"So, it's a dead end."

"I'm afraid so, sir."

"Wonderful and what about the staff who worked there?"

"I've got someone trying to find the director of the establishment, sir."

For an hour, Dravisky poked around Chernekov's dacha, putting his men on edge. When he returned to Moscow, Zahrin looked at the pile of documents on the writing desk that he still had to wade through. He clicked on the desk lamp, bathing the desk in an orange glow. He picked up the first document. It concerned one of Chernekov's Moscow clubs. Slowly he began to read it. Some of this would be relevant, most of it irrelevant. Zahrin's problem was there was only one way to find out, and that was to go through everything.

Chapter 52

The Alexandrian coffee shop was cramped and congested. In the air, the smell of nicotine and caffeine hung oppressively, creating an unhealthy nicotine-caffeine smog. The sound of the customers sucking on the opium pipes at the front of the shop could barely be heard above the noisy, bustling street.

Random chaos, chaos that only Alexandrians seemed capable of, Fasal thought, as he was led through the shop by the greasy-haired coffee shop owner. The others were waiting in the backroom.

The coffee shop owner left. The backroom was stuffy and the smell of tobacco and coffee was even more prominent in the small, congested room.

"Allah, be with you, Fasal," Galdafi, one of the mission's pilots, said, as he stood up to greet him.

"And with you," Fasal said.

They embraced. Fasal did the same with Musharak, the other pilot.

"Are we ready?" Musharak asked.

"I've met Mullah Omah. He wants us ready to move in two weeks," Fasal stated.

"At last," Galdafi said. "We'll soon drive the infidels from our land."

"Allah, be blessed!" Musharak said.

Fasal waited until his colleagues' fervor abated. "One of you will have a passenger with you when we move. I'll also have a passenger in the plane with me."

They looked puzzled. "Why do we have passengers?" Galdafi asked.

"It is necessary. Mullah Omah has decided that, for us to be successful and avoid the infidels meddling in our affairs, then the attack needs to look as if it was instigated by the Jews."

His colleagues still looked puzzled.

"Why is not our concern," Fasal added. "The mission is in the hands of God, we should just count ourselves lucky that we have the chance to do God's work."

Fasal took two sheets of paper from his pocket, on which were written the final details of the plan. He had left it late to tell them. The less they knew, the less chance of a security breach before the big day.

"If the passengers are necessary, then we shall take them," Galdafi conceded.

"You both have to be at the private airfields, at the marked locations, six o'clock the morning of the twenty-ninth of November. At these airfields, you will find hangars where crop dusting Cessnas have been fitted with the biological weapons. Disciples have informed me that the canisters contain enough anthrax agent to contaminate a large area. Many believers will die, but God wills it for the greater good," Fasal stated coldly.

He thought of the squalor and misery that some of them lived in, decided that, in some cases, with their severe poverty levels, it would be a mercy killing.

"Allah's work is never easy," Musharak said, reading through the plan. "And at the airfields, we'll be met by someone?"

"You'll be met," Fasal assured him. "Everything will

be ready. All you'll have to do is follow the instructions and fly the planes."

"And what about this passenger one of us will have with us?" Galdafi asked.

"The passenger will be drugged and already on the plane when you arrive at the airfield," Fasal stated. "There will be a parachute for your use when you're clear of the contaminated area. When you jump from the plane, you're to leave the passenger to be killed when the plane crashes. It's essential that you make sure the passenger looks as if he was flying the plane before you jump."

Galdafi smiled in the certainty that the infamy of such an attack by the infidels could start a Jihad throughout the Arab world. "And am I to be told who the passenger is?"

Fasal hesitated. They were asking Galdafi to risk his life for the cause, the least he could do was tell him who they were. "The two passengers are Jewish fanatics we've kidnapped from the West Bank. They both have pilot's licences. Disciples have planted evidence back in Palestine to implicate the Jews in the attack. When the Muslim world sees what Jewish fanaticism is capable of, then they will unite behind Mullah Omah and the cause."

The pilots considered a moment what lay ahead.

"Once we leave here today will we ever meet again?" Galdafi asked.

Fasal shook his head. "Already we've met too much. Any more meetings would only risk the plot's discovery."

The pilots folded their instructions and put them in their pockets. "Good luck, my friend," Galdafi said and then shook Fasal's hand.

"You leave first, Galdafi, Musharak can follow a few minutes later," Fasal ordered.

The pilots left. Fasal checked the room over and

made sure they'd left nothing behind. Outside, the street was crammed with the usual mishmash of Alexandrian society. Fasal decided that if infidel agents were following him, he'd be unable to spot them in such congestion.

He walked down by the harbor, watching the massed boats bobbing up and down on the dirty green water. He wondered how many of the people he passed as he walked would be alive in a couple of weeks? The decision about who lived or died was out of his hands, once the pilots deployed the weapons. Whoever survived or died, it was the will of God. Only God would decide their fate. Which was the way it should be.

Chapter 53

Director Pravilov, former head of the Sapstondov laboratories, viewed Zahrin's visit to his small apartment with suspicion. The FSB were the KGB, would always be the KGB. It didn't matter what coat they wore or who they pretended to be.

This Zahrin who'd come to see him was a typical example of the new breed. Westernized, trying to look like the CIA. They could try all they liked but they still came across as thugs.

"This consignment, Pravilov, what can you tell me about it?" Zahrin asked.

"It was a long time ago. It's hard to remember." Pravilov decided to go on the defensive. These people could twist things, make them sound like what they weren't.

"It was only eight years ago," Zahrin pressed. "Looking at the dangerous nature of the shipment, I'm sure you'd remember a shipment of *Bacillus Anthracis*."

"How simple the FSB make things sound. A lot has happened since then. I'm now retired and struggling to exist. What happened back then is a distant memory."

"It's important you remember this," Zahrin insisted.

Pravilov sighed. "When I was director at Sapstondov, we were involved in constant research for wonder drugs, drugs that would cure diseases, drugs that would make a fortune for the laboratory that came up with them. For our research, we needed a regular supply of deadly viruses to work on. For the right price, the Stepnogorsk facility in Kazakhstan was only too willing to fly it to us. With the fall of the mighty Soviet system, the Stepnogorsk facility was being starved of government funds, the director was desperate to secure money to keep the establishment functioning."

"We're talking about deadly germ warfare, Pravilov. This is not a commodity that can be sold on the open market."

"You can't blame the director. He wasn't given much choice after the old Soviet funding disappeared. He sought out test laboratories who could pay for his product. How else was he going to keep his facility alive?"

Zahrin couldn't believe what he was hearing. He wondered how many other facilities with big workforces, in desperate need of funding, had sought out desperate solutions. The Communists had left Russia in a mess, and now Zahrin and his colleagues had to try to sort that mess out. "So how many shipments are we talking about?" Zahrin asked with a sense of dread.

"It's difficult to come up with a figure—"

"It's important that you try," Zahrin snapped.

"From the period 1991 until Sapstondov's closure in 1995, I'd say about twenty-five shipments."

"And how big were these shipments?"

Pravilov stared at Zahrin, disbelief etched on his face. "After all these years, and without access to my old facility's records, such a question is impossible to answer."

He had a point, Zahrin decided. The FSB had managed to assemble some of the records from government offices in Rostov-on-Don. The FSB couldn't decipher most of it, maybe Pravilov could.

"I want you to go through the records and see if you can find the relevant shipment. We need to know everything you can remember about this."

"This could take weeks, Zahrin. I still work part time as a research chemist to supplement my pension. I've got a lot of projects I'm working on at the moment."

Zahrin was getting irritated with this weasel of a man. "I've tried to be civil with you, Pravilov. I've tried to get you to do this simple task to help your government, but you keep putting obstacles in the way. I'll give you two choices. Either you cooperate fully with the FSB in this investigation and come out of it with your reputation intact, or you continue with your present attitude, the end result of which will be you being arrested for collaboration with the mafia and charged with the theft of biological weapons."

"This is ridiculous. I know nothing about any of this. You can't charge me for something I know nothing about," Pravilov protested.

"If you don't cooperate, then your non-cooperation will be noted. When some gruesome biological catastrophe caused by these shipped weapons occurs, people are going to blame you, Pravilov," Zahrin promised. "The fact that you refused to help and probably added to any death toll will be noted and taken into account when you have your day in court."

"That's not fair. I'm not responsible for any of this," Pravilov argued.

"If innocent people die, then it's everyone's fault, Director Pravilov," Zahrin said. "If you don't help us, within hours, I'll make sure that the press have the story. You'll be ostracized in your profession."

"That's blackmail."

"Call it what you like. I don't care what you call it. I don't care what you call it, as long as my threats lead to your cooperation."

"It looks like you've given me no choice," Pravilov said.

"I can't afford to give you a choice. There could be millions of lives at stake here."

Pravilov sighed. "I'm going to need access to all the old facility records."

"Good man," Zahrin said.

"The sooner I get on with this, the quicker I get you out my life."

Zahrin led Pravilov to his car. He'd take the scientist back to his office at FSB headquarters and give him access to secure computers.

Pravilov was the key, Zahrin quickly decided. Pravilov was the key to getting to the bottom of this mess.

Chapter 54

The doctor's surgery was grimy and bleak, not the kind of place Chernekov usually went for treatment. He didn't have a choice. The police were after him, the hunt was on. Chernekov was using an underground doctor recommended by a colleague.

Doctor Cassavich looked at the gunshot wound. It was a wound that really should be treated in a hospital.

As Cassavich worked on the wound, Chernekov winced in pain. "Can't you be more fucking careful?" he moaned.

"You should be treated in hospital for such a bad wound," Cassavich said.

"If I could go to hospital, I wouldn't be here."

"Then I'm afraid you'll have to put up with the primitive conditions of my surgery."

Chernekov didn't argue. Pissing off the doctor working on your wound was not a move designed to improve the doctor's workmanship.

"How much longer?" Chernekov asked.

"The wound is severe. You've lost a lot of blood. Normally, in such a case, I'd recommend immediate hospitalisation."

"I can't go to hospital."

"At least give yourself a few days' rest."

"There'll be plenty of time to rest when I'm dead, Doctor. I need to call some people, urgently."

Cassavich could see arguing with this mafia hothead was pointless. "I can give you painkillers and a few dressings to replace the dressing around the stitches. You need to replace the dressing every few days."

Cassavich finished dressing the wound. Chernekov was pleased. "You've done all you can do for me, Doctor. The debt you owed my colleagues for your gambling debts has now been repaid in full."

When Chernekov was dressed, he gently picked up the holdall containing his money and left. Outside, the night air was clear, and a layer of frost enveloped everything. Chernekov pulled the top coat he'd taken from the doctor tight around him. He headed toward the metro on foot. He'd hidden the Mercedes in a side street well away from the surgery office. The police would have an APB out on it, so it was too hot to drive.

He descended the stairs to the metro, quickly lost himself in the bustling crowds. He jumped on a ring line train

The train would take him to Dobryninskaya station. It was an area of the city where he had friends who would hide him. The crowded evening commuters were the perfect cover for his activities. In the cathedral-like stations, Chernekov was just another small insignificant Moscovite going about his business. He had to stand on the train. He felt dizzy and nauseas from his recent loss of blood. He couldn't allow himself to faint. Fainting, and the inevitable kafuffle that would bring, would be his downfall.

When he alighted at Dobryninskaya, he moved slowly and steadily. He went to a long-time colleague's club not far from the station. He entered Balishev's club through a back entrance as a further precaution. The doorman took him to Balishev's office, where a bear-like Balishev sat at his desk counting the takings.

"The whole world is after you," Balishev grumbled, not looking up from his counting.

"That's why I'm here. I need a bed for a couple of days."

"You can't stay here. I bribe the local police to keep away from the club. Your arrival brings too much attention, and, frankly, it's attention I don't need."

"If it wasn't for me warning off my colleagues, telling them that you're under my protection, then you wouldn't have a club."

Balishev finally looked up from what he was doing. He appeared to have come to a decision. "I suppose I owe you something."

"Damn right you do!"

"I'll have a word with Alexi, my doorman. Alexi knows a lot of people. He'll know someone who can put you up for a few days." Balishev momentarily left the room.

Chernekov sat, finally realizing how tired he was. All he needed was a few days' rest and time to think. He thought about Rominev, shocked at how he'd let Rominev get the drop on him. Then there was the FSB assault on his dacha. Why were the FSB suddenly showing him so much attention?

He'd been bribing law enforcement officials for years, and yet there'd still been no advance warning of his impending doom. He wondered if he'd been double-crossed and the bribes hadn't been paid. There were all sorts of things filling his head—things he needed a safe house to sit down in and think about.

Balishev returned. "Alexi knows someone. He'll take you there shortly."

"I need to use a phone," Chernekov said.

Balishev took a mobile phone out of a drawer and slid it across the table to Chernekov. "This phone was left by a customer on a seat. It can't be traced to us, so it's safe to use."

Chernekov stepped out into the corridor to make his calls. The mood of his associates became subdued when they realized the caller was Chernekov. They gave him the cold shoulder, warned him to get out of Moscow. The situation was almost untenable. He felt in his coat pocket for the cold metal reassurance of his Beretta. At the moment, he felt that the gun was the only thing saving him from oblivion.

Outside the club, Alexi said, "My friend lives in a workers' apartment block out by the factories."

Chernekov got into Alexi's car. He decided he was only going to be around long enough to plan his escape abroad. He knew too many secrets of former colleagues for them to let him live. It was only a matter of time before they put out a contract on him. And when that event happened, Chernekov wasn't going to be around to face his former associates' wrath.

Chapter 55

The door opened and light suddenly bathed Stopowitz's prison.

A man put a water bottle and a plate of sandwiches near Stopowitz. The man always kept just far enough away from Stopowitz so he was out of reach. He turned, about to leave.

"I'm not a wealthy man," Stopowitz said quickly. "If you're after a ransom, then you're going to be disappointed."

The man shook his head, as if in disgust. "Is money all you Jews think about? Has it ever occurred to you that there might be another reason why you've been brought here?"

"How long are you going to keep me here?"

"I think, in the interests of your long-term health, you should learn to keep your mouth shut, Jew."

Dravagi left the room. He locked the door and returned to the living room of the house, where a seated Mullah Omah waited.

"How are the prisoners?" Omah asked.

"Stopowitz tried to ask questions. I warned him to keep quiet."

"Remember, Dravagi, I'm holding you personally responsible for their welfare. Without them, we have no mission. You'd do well to remember that."

"I know the delicacy of the situation, master. I'll make sure the men know what's at stake." Dravagi knew what was at stake and that the future of Egypt was in their hands.

"The prisoners have to be fed well. When they arrive at the airfields, they have to be full bellied and show no signs of ill treatment," Omah stated.

"They will be, don't worry, master," Dravagi said.

Omah sat staring at Dravagi. To Dravagi, it looked like he was contemplating some deep philosophical question.

It was the mystique of the man that had drawn Dravagi to him as a follower. When you compared Omah to the weak corrupt politicians that inhabited Egyptian politics, then it was obvious to Dravagi that Omah was the way to the future.

"Very well, Dravagi, I won't insult you by mentioning this matter again."

Omah leaned forward so he was close to the nearby table. On the table was a detailed map of Northern Egypt. On the map, the airfields where the Cessnas would be taking off from were marked. Omah studied the map intently, smiling when his fingers ran across the airfields.

He was pleased. "The planes will take off at six o'clock in the morning a week from today. This will be our last meeting before then. If you have any questions, ask them now, Dravagi."

"I have no questions. I understand what's required of me, master."

Fasal entered the room. "You wanted to see me, Mullah Omah?"

"The fate of everything relies on you pilots, Fasal. When you parachute from the planes, you have to make it look like the Jews were flying them. The success of the plan depends on there being no doubt that the Jews carried out the attack."

"I understand, master," Fasal said.

"In the confusion and blame that will follow the attack, our followers will seize power. The people will welcome our strong leadership and stand against the Jews. Allah, be praised!"

"God is great!" Dravagi said.

"We must be vigilant, my brothers. Government agents are always looking to infiltrate so they can annihilate us," Omah warned.

They went through the plan in fine detail. When certain that they all understood everything, they shook hands, and Omah left. Fasal and Dravagi embraced each other. The moment of destiny was almost upon them. Fasal left soon after. As he walked along the dusty streets past fluttering washing on balconies, he wondered how many of the children carelessly playing in the street would survive the attack.

He headed out of Islamic Cairo and back toward Garden City and his hotel. Fasal was finding it hard to look any pedestrian in the eye. Since his meeting with Omah, they all looked like ghosts to him now. He accidentally bumped into a woman carrying a shopping bag. She cursed him then hurried off.

Back in his hotel room, as Fasal lay on his bed trying to sleep, he couldn't get the picture of the woman's haggard face out of his head. When he'd looked into the woman's tired yellow-flecked eyes, it was like looking into the eyes of the walking dead.

Chapter 56

Karishen sensed something was wrong when the sour-faced Russian customs officer, who had already let several people through the gate, put his hand up for Karishen and his girlfriend to stop.

"Come with me, please," he ordered.

The formal tone of the customs officer's voice told Karishen that this wasn't routine but something more. "Is something wrong, officer?" he asked nervously.

"Just routine, sir," the officer said, opening a side door which led to the interview rooms.

As they entered the corridor where two FSB men waited, Karishen suddenly realized this was anything *but* routine. He was led to an interview room where Zahrin waited.

The officer told Karishen and Natasha to sit on the uncomfortable chairs.

"This is outrageous," Karishen said. "Why are we being detained?"

"Everything will become clear shortly, Mr. Karishen," Zahrin said. "Let's start with your dealings with Mr. Chernekov."

"Who?" Karishen said.

"We've got evidence, Karishen. We know you've been taking bribes from him, and, in return, you have allowed certain cargoes through St Petersburg."

Zahrin was used to interrogation. Karishen was sweating, looking uncomfortable in his chair. He looked a weak man—a man, Zahrin decided, who could be easily broken.

"I don't know what you're talking about," Karishen offered weakly. "In my job as assistant harbor master of St Petersburg, I deal with countless people daily. I might have had dealings with this man, but if I did, I don't remember them."

"Let me refresh your memory. Mr. Chernekov is a member of the Russian mafia. Mr. Chernekov is wanted for many crimes and is currently on the run after a shootout at his dacha, a shootout where two FSB officers were killed. As you can imagine, my colleagues are extremely pissed off with Chernekov and anybody associated with him. That makes you a pretty unpopular fellow among the FSB, Karishen."

Natasha bit her lip. "Do you know this Chernekov, Boris?"

"Like I said, I encounter so many people in my work. It's impossible to remember them all."

"Don't be silly, Karishen. Do you really think we'd be interviewing you if we didn't have the evidence to back up our charges?" Zahrin turned to Natasha. "How do you think he's able to take you on luxury weekends to places like Helsinki? Where do you think a man on a deputy harbor master's salary gets all this money for luxury weekends?"

Karishen swallowed hard. "I'm sure this is just a misunderstanding. I've never met this Chernekov. If I had, I'd remember it."

"Do you remember meeting a man called, Rominev?

You met him in a truckers' café just off the St Petersburg highway."

"I've no idea what you're talking about—"

Zahrin banged his fist hard on the table. "Don't be stupid. I've had a man tailing you. I know everything you've been doing." Zahrin lifted a briefcase from beneath the table and laid it on the table. From inside he took out some photos and placed them in front of Karishen.

Karishen looked at the photos, his face slowly registering horror as he viewed the pictures of him meeting Rominev.

Zahrin pointed at some photos. "These photos are of Rominev entering and leaving Chernekov's dacha. They were taken on the same night you met Rominev."

Karishen stared at the pictures.

"And the photos to your left show you meeting Rominev in the truckers' café."

Zahrin sat back and let Karishen contemplate his fate.

Karishen came to a decision. "I'm not saying another thing until I have a lawyer present."

"I'll get you a phone. You can have a lawyer," Zahrin said. "When we've finished here, you'll be arrested for your part in Chernekov's smuggling operations. I have to warn you, Karishen, you might be facing much more than just an aiding smuggling charge. I'm afraid we've uncovered evidence that Chernekov was smuggling consignments of weapons from research laboratories, and he's been using St. Petersburg to smuggle these weapons out on freighters."

Karishen's face suddenly came alive with tension.

Zahrin decided Karishen was finally aware of the gravity of what he was involved in. "In light of the terrorist threat worldwide, you can see what an alarming development this is. If the shipments you've been involved in contained biological weapons and are used by terrorists in a genocidal attack, then you'll be facing charges of mass murder."

Karishen thought the shipments had been drugs—not this, never this. He wondered how much and how far the FSB could trace things. He'd rented a safety deposit box, never actually had large sums of money in his account. The FSB's powers were wide and far-reaching. It was only a matter of time before they found the safety deposit box. The game was up. He decided the time to be obstructive was over. If he didn't cooperate, God only knew what charges they'd throw at him. "I never knew it was biological weapons. I just thought he was smuggling contraband goods."

Zahrin decided to be conciliatory. He'd found that conciliation could have some startlingly positive results in interviews. "You don't seem like such a bad guy, Karishen. I can see that Chernekov suckered you into working for him. The Russian mafia are good at assessing a man's weakness." He looked across at Natasha and smiled. "Your mistress is your weakness. You wanted to show her a good time. To do that you needed money. Chernekov obviously played on that fact. The mafia are good at finding a man's vulnerabilities."

Karishen felt like the bastard had read his mind. If he knew the situation so well, if he could see how Karishen had been suckered in, maybe there was the possibility of a deal. "So where does all this leave me?"

"This is major crime, Karishen. I can't promise you a lot, but I'll promise you one thing—if you cooperate fully with the FSB investigation, then I'll see that the courts know of it and that it's taken into account when they sentence you."

"Not good enough. The price I put on my cooperation is that you keep Natasha out of all of this."

"We're not interested in your mistress. If you cooperate, she doesn't need to be involved in any of this."

Karishen turned to Natasha. "I'm sorry you've been involved in any of this, darling. I only took the bribes because I wanted to give you the best that money can buy."

Karishen and Natasha hugged briefly, then she kissed him.

"Natasha is an innocent bystander. If you cooperate, we won't be charging her with anything," Zahrin reassured him.

"Okay, if Natasha isn't charged, and you put in a good word for me, then I'll tell you everything."

Zahrin stood. "We'll start by going to your office and studying old cargo manifests. We need to know when and where the shipments, went."

"Could I speak to Natasha alone for a few minutes?" Karishen asked.

"Of course you can."

Zahrin knew when to offer the carrot and not beat the stick. He left them alone. After few brief minutes, when they were done, the FSB and Karishen had some serious work to do.

Chapter 57

Chernekov sat in the grim, damp room he was sleeping in at the hideout. He made many calls on the mobile he'd been given by Balishev. As the day wore on and all the replies from his former gangland colleagues were negative, he quickly concluded he was a social leper and had to react accordingly.

Before he finally left Moscow for good, he dialed one last number and arranged one last thing, a hit on Rominev.

Vassilov charged him $100,000 for it—vastly overcharged him. It made his blood boil to think how former colleagues were now cashing in on his misfortune.

He heard someone slipping a key into the lock of the front door. He moved along the dusty corridor with his Beretta in his hand, ready. Buterin opened the front door. Buterin was the owner of the flat he was hiding in. Chernekov lowered his gun and stepped back so Buterin could enter.

Buterin entered and shut the door. In his hands, he carried Chinese takeaway food bags. He went to the kitchen and put the bags on a table. "I thought you might like a proper meal for a change." He took two tins of beer from the fridge and got some plates and cutlery from the drawer. "I'm going to have a shower first. Help yourself. I'll have mine later."

Buterin went to the bathroom. A starving Chernekov spooned some food onto a plate. He sat at the kitchen table and ate ravenously. This meal was the first proper meal he'd eaten in days. He swigged some beer, and suddenly felt sharp penetrating pains in his stomach. He wondered if it was aftershock from the shooting? A reaction to losing so much blood. He tried to stand. His head was dizzy, and he couldn't move his legs. Chernekov fell to the floor in a state of paralysis. As he lay on the cold tiled floor waiting for Buterin to return, his vision became blurred and out of focus.

At last Buterin entered the kitchen, Chernekov couldn't help noticing Buterin was dry and still wearing the same clothes he'd gone to the shower in. It was at this point that Chernekov knew.

He tried to stand, but the power to move his body had been lost due to the paralysing effect of the poison. He gasped one final time for breath before his face suddenly became a death mask.

Buterin cautiously walked over to Chernekov's body and checked for life signs. When satisfied that Chernekov was dead, he took out his mobile phone and made a call. "He's dead," he told Balishev. "I need the clean-up team to come and remove the body."

"They'll be with you within the hour," Balishev promised.

Buterin looked out the window at the dark winter evening. The cold and dark were the perfect time to move the body. Buterin had just redecorated his kitchen, so there was going to be no cutting up of the body in here. However they disposed of Chernekov's body, it was going to be well away from Buterin's flat. He would make sure of it.

Chapter 58

Zahrin sat at Karishen's desk, looking at what Karishen had been up to recently on his computer. They were trawling through cargo shipments. Karishen paused at the cargo bound for Haifa, Israel, on the container ship, *Vladimar*.

"This container shipment of agricultural parts was the most recent cargo that Chernekov bribed me to allow through customs," Karishen said.

"It says agricultural parts. If it wasn't checked, then we've no idea what was inside the container." Zahrin didn't like to think about extremists getting hold of biological weapons. It was even more dangerous when those extremists came from a particularly volatile region such as the Middle East.

Standing behind Karishen and Zahrin, Ravillidi, the customs officer assigned to help the FSB with the investigation, looked over their shoulders at the screen. "It obviously isn't agricultural parts," he said, stating the obvious.

"The manifest said it arrived in Haifa two days ago. By now, the contents of the container will be long gone," Zahrin grumbled.

"I'll get onto Haifa and ask them about it," Ravillidi said. He left the room to accomplish the task.

"I want details of every single cargo you've allowed through for Chernekov, Karishen. Hold back anything, and the deal is off."

"There've only been three cargoes. I've only been doing it for a few months. Apart from the Haifa shipment, there was a cargo to Ireland and one to France."

"And how much did Chernekov pay you for letting these cargoes through?" Zahrin asked.

"He paid twenty thousand dollars for each cargo."

Zahrin whistled. "It must have been something very important for him to pay such a bribe."

"I thought it was for contraband goods he was trying to avoid paying customs levies on." Karishen realized how feeble his protestations sounded, but what else did he have?

"So you never thought it was drugs, guns, or biological weapons?" Zahrin asked. "Weren't you suspicious of the cargo to Ireland? Didn't it enter your head that the cargo for Ireland might be weapons for terrorists?"

"If I'd thought it was any of these, I'd never have gotten involved," Karishen lied.

He was smitten with Natasha and needed money to keep her. Karishen knew he was an overweight balding petty official. He was realistic and knew that the only way of keeping Natasha in his life was by giving her the things she couldn't get with guys her own age.

"Bollocks! You'd have taken the money, whatever the cargo." Zahrin had noted in his FSB career that people only seemed to have a conscience after they were caught.

"Is that how you regard me, Zahrin? I've got friends and family. Do you really think I want to be the instigator of a biological war that might kill my loved ones?"

"I think your head is ruled by your prick," Zahrin said. "I think you'd do anything to keep a young bit of pussy in your life."

"You probably won't believe me, Zahrin, but I love Natasha."

"Well, she won't love you when this is over. You've made a real fucking mess of your life. Your marriage is over. You were in a position of trust and you abused it, Karishen. When this is over, even with the good word I'll put in for you, you'll have to spend time in prison." Zahrin paused to let the magnitude of what awaited Karishen sink in. "Natasha is young. She'll quickly move on. When you look back and analyse all this, Karishen, you have to ask yourself was it worth it?"

Karishen's silence told Zahrin it wasn't.

Ravillidi returned to Karishen's office. "The Israelis say that the containers off the *Vladimar* have all cleared customs and left the port of Haifa. After I told them what we've discovered, they've put every man they've got on it."

"At least they're listening," Zahrin said.

"There's a problem. Haifa wasn't the only port of call. There was a stop in Alexandria in Egypt. All the cargoes unloaded there are accounted for. Customs say that they checked everything that came off the ship. They say that, but Karishen is proof of the fact that officials can be bribed, so we can't be certain of anything."

"That's all we need," Zahrin moaned as he suddenly realized the search field had widened.

"I'm now going to get on the phone to Alexandria and warn them what we've discovered." Ravillidi left the room to contact Alexandria.

"You write down everything you know about all three cargoes you were bribed to let through," Zahrin told Karishen. "I don't want any more surprises."

Karishen was careful what he wrote. He was particularly worried about the Irish cargo. If it was a shipment of terrorist weapons, he could be in a lot more trouble. Karishen stopped writing. "I've finished."

Zahrin grabbed the paper and briefly read Karishen's notes. "What a fucking mess."

Karishen couldn't agree more. He was getting more worried. He could see no way he was ever going to extricate himself from this.

Chapter 59

Customs officer Mosha Shavbiz eyed the farmhouse through powerful binoculars. Was it possible that the consignment of tractor parts delivered here was, in fact, biological weapons? He'd been watching the farm for a couple of hours, and there was no sign of any activity. It was time to move in.

He spoke to his colleague Benin on the walkie-talkie. "Move in!" Shavbiz ordered.

Suddenly, a team of men descended on the farm. The farmer was bewildered by all the agents that arrived at his door. Shavbiz showed the farmer his ID. The farmer and his family seemed genuinely shocked by an armed unit dressed in biological weapons suits hammering at their door.

"I'm from Israeli customs, my colleague there is Inspector Steiner of the police," Shavbiz stated.

"What's the meaning of this?" the startled farmer asked, while his wife protectively held their young son.

"You've had a consignment of agricultural parts delivered to your farm recently, Mr. Perrez."

"Yes, it's no secret. All the stuff I ordered has been cleared through customs. There wasn't a problem—"

"Can I see the consignment?" Shavbiz asked.

"Have I got a choice?" Perrez asked.

Shavbiz handed Perrez a court order allowing the search of the premises. "None at all."

Officers cautiously began the search. Perrez showed the police the tractor parts stored in a barn. There was no sign of any biological weapons. The agents took the Perrez family into custody. They handcuffed Perrez and put him under armed guard. After a thorough search, the search team had come up with nothing.

In an interview room at a Haifa lower city police station, Perrez sat nervously. Shavbiz, Steiner, and Benin sat menacingly opposite.

"It'll be easier for you and your family if you tell us where the canisters are," Shavbiz said.

"I've no idea what you're talking about," Perrez said.

"The biological warfare canisters that were hidden in the consignment of tractor parts you ordered." Shavbiz wasn't getting the results from the interview he hoped for and Perrez looked genuinely dumbfounded.

"I only received tractor spares. The stuff you're looking for is obviously dangerous. There's no way I'd ever endanger my family by bringing lethal weapons to the farm."

"Just tell us where you've hidden them," Shavbiz pressed. "We'll be lenient if you cooperate."

Perrez leaned back defiantly in his chair and stared blankly at them. "I don't know anything about this. Whatever you're looking for, I'm not involved in it."

"The container with the weapons in it was delivered to your farm in a consignment of tractor parts," Benin stated. "Given that as a fact, then you're our most likely suspect, Perrez."

In the last two years, Perrez had bad crops. It meant he had to look for cheaper engine part suppliers than usual, which had led him to the tractor factory in Russia.

"When I unloaded those tractor parts in my yard, there were no biological canisters in that container," Perrez said.

Steiner beckoned Shavbiz outside, in the corridor. "We didn't find any trace of the biological weapons at the farm," Steiner said. "We did find these, though."

Steiner showed Shavbiz some extreme anti-Arab propaganda leaflets. "And these were at the farm?" Shavbiz asked.

"There are bags full of them hidden in the barn's loft."

Shavbiz took the leaflets back into the interview room to show Perrez, laying them out on the table in front of him. "It appears that you're more active in political circles than you're letting on, Mr. Perrez."

"I've never seen those leaflets before in my life," Perrez exclaimed.

"They were hidden in the loft of your barn, Mr. Perrez." Shavbiz looked at Perrez's face for a reaction but all he saw was incomprehension.

"I didn't put them there," Perrez protested angrily.

Shavbiz looked at one of the leaflets, tutting as he read them. "There's a lot you don't seem to know, Mr. Perrez. You don't seem to know, yet everything we've uncovered seems to point an accusatory finger at you."

"I've done nothing, I know nothing," Perrez shouted. "I'm not saying another word until I get a lawyer."

"Have it your way, Mr. Perrez," Shavbiz responded.

When the lawyer arrived, Steiner and Shavbiz took the interview chairs opposite Perrez and his lawyer, Yashina.

"If your client doesn't fully cooperate, Mr. Yashina, then the State of Israel will assume that he's actively involved in biological terrorism," Steiner said.

Yashina surprised Steiner by smiling. "Let me be

clear, Inspector," he said. "My client ordered Russian tractor parts. However, it appears that criminals may have used this container to smuggle biological weapons into Israel. My client is a man with an unblemished character, and is now under threat of incarceration solely because he was an easy target for smugglers."

"The extremist settler leaflets we found hidden in the loft on your client's farm shows your client is politically active with extreme settler sects," Steiner said.

"My client says he knows nothing of the leaflets, nor does he have any idea who put them there. From what I can see, my client has committed no crime, and you have no evidence of him committing one. All you have is evidence that someone might have used a container of tractor parts he was having delivered to smuggle biological weapons into Israel," Yashina responded.

Steiner had already taken a dislike to Yashina, whom he saw as a typical smug lawyer with an attitude. Yashina was the type of man who made a policeman's life impossible. Steiner could see that they had a long session ahead of them. If the canisters had been smuggled into Israel, using Perrez's container, then time was against them. Every second wasted could be a second closer to some fanatic using them. It then left—

Steiner didn't want to contemplate what it left.

Chapter 60

Just after nightfall, a tired, hungry Steiner arrived at a Jerusalem police station. He quickly found the detectives' section, where slim athletic Inspector Slemen awaited him. Slemen led Steiner to his office, where he pointed Steiner to a chair, and they both sat.

"I was alarmed at what you told me, Steiner. Are you certain this container was carrying biological weapons?" Slemen asked him.

"As certain as we can be. The Russians found links to shipments of *Bacillus Anthracis* canisters from a Russian biological weapons center in Stepnegorsk, Kazakhstan. These canisters were shipped to a research laboratory in southern Russia," Steiner added. "When the FSB raided the dacha of a Russian mafia big wig, they found he'd been involved in smuggling biological weapons out of Russia. Evidence suggests some might have been sent to Israel."

"Our worst nightmare, if the PLO got hold of such weapons."

"Precisely, which is why I'm here," Steiner said. "I don't think you have to worry about the PLO, Slemen. The evidence we've uncovered actually points to Jewish extremists."

"I've investigated the sect mentioned in the leaflets stored in Perrez's barn, and the leader of the sect, Leon Stopowitz, and his lieutenant, Cohen, have disappeared. The settlers claim that Stopowitz and Cohen have been murdered by the Palestinians." Slemen looked at a file on his desk. "They disappeared on the road to Jerusalem about a week ago. We haven't recovered their bodies."

"Very convenient, Slemen. Our two main suspects disappearing just before the suspect container arrives in Haifa."

"We'd better search Stopowitz's settlement." Slemen picked up the phone and called some people to put things in motion. "The settlement is surrounded by two Palestinian villages which are separated by an army checkpoint, hardly an ideal place to smuggle biological canisters into."

When Slemen, Steiner, and their search team arrived at the Stopowitz home, Dinah Stopowitz was irate. "Why are you searching my home? Why aren't you out there looking for Leon?"

"I'm sorry, Mrs. Stopowitz, but, in light of recent developments, we have no choice but to search this community," Slemen responded, showing her the search warrant.

"What developments?" she enquired.

"I'm afraid, as of this moment, I'm not at liberty to tell you that, Mrs. Stopowitz." Slemen intended telling her as little as possible, fearing she might let something slip.

"But you're at liberty to tear my home to pieces? You tear my home to pieces while the Palestinians have kidnapped and possibly murdered Leon. Instead of searching their communities, you search ours."

"If we find nothing, I'll make sure my men put everything back the way they found it."

A police woman took Dinah Stopowitz outside. Apart from some troubling anti-Muslim literature, and a detailed map of future proposed Jewish settlements on the West Bank the sect planned on building without government permission, there were no signs of biological weapons.

Steiner stepped outside. Slemen joined him.

Steiner couldn't mask the apprehension he knew was etched on his tired, lined face. "A dead end."

"It was a long shot," Slemen said.

They returned to their car. "If they're involved in smuggling these weapons into Israel, you can be sure they've gone to elaborate lengths to cover their tracks," Steiner added.

"Maybe the FSB are wrong about the sect having weapons," Slemen said.

When the pair had left, after finding nothing during their three-hour search, Slemen contemplated what had transpired as he eased their vehicle into heavy highway traffic.

Steiner also reflected as Slemen drove. Maybe they were wrong—perhaps they were filling in the gaps to satisfy their own apocalyptic theories. He thought of the hateful speeches the Jewish extremists had directed at the Palestinians in recent years and had little doubt these fanatics, in their misguided sense of working for God, were capable of mass murder. It was a thought he couldn't remove from his mind, one that made him determined to carry on until he found out the truth.

Chapter 61

Chief Inspector Pasha of the Alexandria police was standing on the Alexandria Harbor quayside, talking to the harried-looking unloading foreman.

The foreman paused from looking at the paperwork he held in front of him. "The ship did unload some of its cargo here, Chief Inspector. However, all of it was unloaded in accordance with the customs regulations."

Pasha pictured the usual Alexandrian chaos when the dock men unloaded a ship. It would be virtually impossible to keep track of anything. "I want to interview everybody involved."

"That's impossible, Chief Inspector. Most of the staff we employ are casual. They move around, looking for work," the foreman explained.

"Then give me the names and addresses of all the regulars you know about," Pasha demanded.

"Come with me," the foreman said.

Pasha and his colleague, Sergeant Casarak, followed the foreman through bales of Egyptian cotton waiting on the quayside to be loaded on a ship. They arrived at a small office behind a warehouse. Pasha and Casarak went inside where Ahmed Kalhid, manager of Alexandria Globofreight, sat. Sweat was dripping off Kalhid's thin lined face. Kalhid's portly build was obviously accentuated by spending too much time in his poorly ventilated office and not doing enough exercise.

He looked up from his desk, eying his visitors suspiciously. "What can I do for you gentlemen?"

"Two weeks ago the Russian container ship *Vladimar* berthed here and unloaded some containers. We want to know everything about them," Pasha said.

Kalhid laughed. "Two weeks is a lifetime in the port life of Alexandria." He pointed to a pile of paperwork perched on the corner of his worn desk. "That's the paperwork I've got to sort out from this week's cargoes. All of it has to be crosschecked with the computer—"

"I don't need a lecture. Just tell me all the people you know who were involved in unloading the containers off the *Vladimar*," Pasha demanded.

Kalhid looked on his computer and found the *Vladimar* cargo manifest. "Fifty containers were unloaded off the ship. I'll print out details of what each container had in them." He printed out the containers' details, handed the printout to Pasha, then went to a filling cabinet. From the cabinet, he took out a sheet of paper from a file. On the paper was a list of the regular port workers who were involved in unloading the containers. "These are my regulars, the men I always use for cargo unloading work. The employment of casual labor is something I don't get involved in. I leave the employment of casual labour to the unloading foreman."

He handed the worksheet for unloading the *Vladimar* to Pasha. Kalhid explained the unloading procedure while Casarak took notes. Pasha looked at the sheet and considered what this all meant.

He tied in what he'd learned from Kalhid with what he'd been told by the Russians.

"Do you think a container bound for Haifa could've

been unloaded and opened in Alexandria, then put back on the *Vladimar*?" Pasha asked.

"In the chaos of an Alexandria quayside, anything is possible, Inspector." Kalhid reflected. "Globofreight is always having things pilfered from our cargoes, but I'm talking about crates being opened and maybe the odd TV being stolen. What you're talking about is much more complex. To take a container off a ship involves a crane, a crane driver, and would involve several people on the quayside unloading the container before it was lifted back on the ship."

"Who are the crane drivers on this list?" Pasha asked.

Kalhid looked at the sheet and pointed them out. Pasha looked at the names but had already decided that he would interview the crane drivers first. Pasha thanked Kalhid, and the policemen took their paperwork and left.

When they'd gone, Kalhid took out his mobile phone and called his contact. "The police have been asking questions."

"Stay calm. They don't know anything," the contact said.

"They were asking about the *Vladimar*," Kalhid stated. He could feel the tension on the other end of the line.

"Don't say anything, everything is under control," the contact reassured him then hung up.

Kalhid sat back in his chair. His back was sweating intensely, and he realized that, today, the sweat wasn't just because of the heat, but was a mixture of sweat and nerves. Culani, the crane driver, would remain silent. They paid him well for unloading the container. The threat of prison if Culani broke his silence would surely guarantee it. Culani also had a family and knew the heavy price his family would pay if he broke his code of silence.

At moments like this, Kalhid wondered whether it

had been wise to take a bribe from the extremists for allowing the container to be unloaded. The money had been too good to refuse. The chance of a quick financial killing had made the temptation impossible to resist.

With the police closing in, the risk now seemed to far outweigh the reward. Kalhid would ignore what work he had planned for the afternoon. Only one thing now mattered in his shady existence. Covering his tracks was all he intended to concentrate on for the moment. He would have to cover up his part in this whole business well. For, if the authorities found a link between Kalhid and the extremists, retribution would be swift and brutal.

Chapter 62

Rominev sat soaking up the sun on the veranda of his luxury villa gracing the lush Montego Bay hillside. He sipped his rum, watching the rippling white waves lapping against the soft white sand of the bay. Rominev could understand how Ian Fleming chose to write his books here. Who could not relax in this perfect tranquillity?

He thought of dreary Moscow. The snow would now be in the city, causing the populace to reach for the vodka bottle. Winter in Moscow was a season Rominev would hopefully never see again in his lifetime. Returning to his homeland was an impossibility. His work with Chernekov and the mafia now meant he'd permanently severed ties to his homeland. He jumped in his hired Renault and headed into town.

He had phone calls to make, supplies to buy. He found a phone box near a restaurant in the touristy side of town.

His sister answered quickly. "Where have you been, Miloslav?" she asked. "Your colleagues have been asking about you. They interrogated me at your station."

"And what did you tell them?"

She laughed. "What should I have told them? Should

I tell them that you're a brother who rarely comes to see me? Should I tell them that, when you do, you're always in a hurry to depart?"

"I've had problems with the mafia. It's safer if I keep away from you and get out of Moscow for a while."

"Ever since the interrogation, I've been worried about you, Miloslav. If I knew where you were, it would help."

"Don't worry. Everything will be okay. I'm just staying out the way for a while. I'll talk to you again when things cool down."

"What do I tell the police if they come back to me?"

"Don't tell them anything. Just keep repeating you don't know anything."

"Well, I don't." Her voice grew agitated.

"That's the spirit." Rominev joked.

"If it's what you want, it's what I'll do. I still think you're being ridiculous though, Miloslav."

"You've always said that, by never settling down, I'm stupid, babushka. My actions just prove how right you were."

"Goodbye, Miloslav."

Rominev hung up. He didn't dawdle on his calls. His experience with Kranjenkov's fuck ups showed it didn't pay to dawdle. That would be the last call to his sister for a while.

Keeping in touch with his family was a luxury he couldn't afford.

Back in Moscow, Vassilov pressed the button on his computer call-tracking device. In a few seconds, all the digits of the number from which Rominev had called appeared. The call had come from a pay phone in Montego Bay, Jamaica. Moments later, Vassilov was on his mobile phone, making travel plans.

Chapter 63

Pasha listened to Culani the crane driver's wooden account of unloading the cargo. Culani seemed visibly to sweat more when Pasha started questioning him about the container they were interested in. After years on the police force, Pasha was a good reader of men, and he knew that Culani's nervous disposition meant he was lying.

"All the containers look the same, Chief Inspector. I just unload what I'm asked to."

"This one was different. This container you personally unloaded. Something was removed, then later you put it back on the ship." Pasha said roughly.

"I never put anything back on the ship," Culani said.

Pasha decided he'd denied it too quickly, concluding the man wasn't much of an actor. "That's the answer I'd expect if you were paid by someone to remove a container then put it back on the ship," Pasha said.

Culani decided he had no other options other than to keep denying the whole thing. "I've already told you, I just unload what I'm told to unload."

Pasha pulled out a search warrant from his pocket and showed it to Culani. "This is a warrant from the courts, allowing me to search your home."

Sergeant Casarak and a couple of officers began the search. A flustered Culani turned on Pasha. "Why are you searching my home? I've been answering your questions. I'm cooperating."

In the other room, Mrs. Culani argued with the search team. Pasha ordered Culani to go and get his wife. Culani started toward the other room and Pasha observed his movements. As he entered the hall, Culani tried to grab something from a potted plant. Once Culani had the item in his hand, Pasha grabbed him, wrestling the item away—a wad of American bank notes banded tightly together with an elastic band.

"There's a lot of money in crane driving these days," Pasha remarked sarcastically.

"It's money I've been saving to buy my wife a surprise anniversary present," Culani said.

"Count it, Casarak," Pasha ordered, "and lay the money out on this coffee-table."

Casarak did as requested and counted the money, which came to over a thousand dollars. "You must've saved five years without eating to save this amount," Pasha scoffed.

"I won some of the money at cards."

Pasha laughed. "It seems you have an answer for everything, Culani, but soon your answers are going to run out. When that happens, you're going to have some serious explaining to do."

"I've told you what the money was for," Culani continued.

"Ridiculous. Nobody in your position has this kind of money." Pasha could see Culani's face redden, realizing that he had him on the ropes.

"I've nothing more to say on the matter."

The search was complete. Apart from the money, the police found nothing. Pasha turned to Casarak. "I want

Mr. Culani taken in for questioning, Sergeant."

"I've told you everything I know," Culani protested.

"Not everything," Pasha said. "That money says that you've done something outside the law. I need to know what that is."

When seated in the interview room at the station Culani looked more forlorn than he had at the house. "I haven't done anything."

"That money tells me something different. That money tells me you've been involved in some kind of smuggling enterprise. I think you were paid to unofficially unload a container off the ship *Vladimar* two weeks ago." Pasha noticed Culani shifting uneasily in his seat. "If you don't want to go to prison, you're going to have to tell me who paid you to take the tractor parts container off the *Vladimar*."

"I've no idea what you're talking about," Culani retorted nervously.

"I think you know exactly what I'm talking about," Pasha prompted. "I think you're too scared to rat on whoever put you up to this. You're scared of retribution and, rightfully, worried about your family."

Culani lapsed into silence. Pasha got Culani a coffee then left the room, giving Culani time to mull over his situation.

"It must be him, sir," Casarak said. "Nobody has that kind of money in his lowly paid job."

"I want you to check out all Globofreight employees. I want to know the internal company workings, who was in a position to have been involved with the dodgy container."

Casarak left to obey Pasha's orders, and Pasha returned to his office. He sat in his chair thinking. Moments later, Chief of Police Alabi arrived in Pasha's office.

"Any progress?" Alabi asked.

"The crane driver had over a thousand dollars hidden in his house," Pasha stated. "He definitely has something to do with it."

"Do you think the fundamentalists could've got hold of the canisters?"

"I don't know, sir. The reports we've got from Israel say the canisters were unloaded in Haifa, but that doesn't explain Culani's money."

"What do I tell the government?" Alabi asked. "I'm being hounded by them. The Americans want to know what happened to the Russian biological weapons."

"I think Culani will crack if we pressure him, sir. If he's involved with the fundamentalists, he's probably too scared to talk."

Alabi was tired of fighting the extremists. Islamic militants were like a cancer spreading over Egypt. The poverty and slums of Cairo and Alexandria were the perfect breeding ground. Alabi decided he didn't have enough to satisfy the government, but it was all he had. He left the room to ring his government liaison. He'd tell them what they had, which, at the moment, was almost nothing.

Chapter 64

Vassilov was in a government office in Montego Bay going through the records for recently rented property and land purchases. The bribed official had left the room, leaving Vassilov alone with the files. There were possibilities. Montego Bay was dotted with rental properties, and if Rominev had rented one of them, Vassilov would find him.

There was so much ground to cover and so little to go on. Vassilov was using the alias of a private detective. He was supposed to be tracking down an estranged husband who'd fled Russia with his assets to avoid a massive divorce settlement. After handing over fifty dollars to the clerk, he was willing to let Vassilov look at the lists of people renting properties.

In the dark world of murder and assassination, you were only as good as your last job. Vassilov's last job had been extremely successful. His last hit had killed the director of the defense sector holding company with one shot from a hundred meters.

Vassilov was expensive. In Chernekov's case, he'd been very expensive. Chernekov was in no position to argue. Vassilov had charged more than his usual fee, as he knew that Chernekov was desperate and without friends. A man with no friends in the Russian underworld has no choice but to pay. When you hired Vassilov, he guaranteed you success.

Vassilov's legendary efficiency meant you could never link the kill back to the hirer. He studied the list of names of foreigners renting villas on the island. The majority of the villas were rented out to holiday travelers, the names recorded. If Rominev was in Montego Bay, Vassilov would find him.

Vassilov drove his hired car to a Yardie-run fisherman's shop overlooking Kingston's dazzling harbor. He parked away from the shop. In his business, you always took precautions.

As he entered the shop, the surly looking black guy behind the counter asked, "You want something, boss?"

"I'm looking for hunting equipment—rifles and pistols," was the reply.

The shop owner was immediately suspicious. "We only have fishing equipment in this store, boss."

Vassilov moved closer. "A mutual friend of ours, Tara, told me I can purchase a handgun here."

"And how much did your friend say you could buy a handgun for?" the shopkeeper asked warily.

"For an untraceable handgun, a thousand dollars is the going rate."

"Your friend seems to know a lot." The shopkeeper looked Vassilov suspiciously up and down. He came to a decision. "Okay, boss, you follow me out the back."

Out the back, the shopkeeper produced several pistols. "I want the money up front," he demanded.

The shopkeeper cautiously kept the ammo away from the pistols. Although the strange Russian had used the secret Yardie Tara code, the shopkeeper still didn't trust him.

Vassilov took the money from his wallet and laid it

on the table next to the weapons. "I want the Beretta 92F, but I want a snap-on suppressor with it."

"The suppressor will cost you another three hundred, boss."

Extorting bastard, Vassilov thought. He considered using his sambo skills to kill the bastard, but decided it wouldn't be practical as it would cause too much rumpus in the local gangland community. He decided the repercussions in Moscow from his mafia contact would be swift and merciless, if they found out Vassilov had killed the Yardie gun dealer they'd put him in contact with.

He handed the shopkeeper three hundred more and snapped, "This gun had better be good."

"All my guns are good, boss." The shopkeeper smiled. "You wouldn't be here if they weren't."

Vassilov slipped the suppressor on the gun. He tested the mechanism, quickly concluding the gun was as good as the dealer said it was. Vassilov slipped the gun into a sports holdall. The dealer nervously handed Vassilov a couple of boxes of ammunition.

They returned to the shop and Vassilov left. He drove out of Kingston. A few miles out, he pulled onto a secluded dirt road, where, at a shaded clearing, he tested the pistol out, firing a round at a rusted can he'd spotted at the side of the track. After missing the first, shot he made some adjustments and fired several more shots which were all on target.

Weapon adjustment was always difficult. All handguns came off production lines and were meant to be manufactured the same, but, to the pro, every gun was slightly different.

He put the gun away then studied a map of the island. He picked out the nearest rented properties to his current position. The nearest was about a mile up the road. As he drove, he stared at the wonderful lush green palm trees and clear blue sea. A stark contrast to the pollution of Moscow he'd recently left behind him. He thought this would be a wonderful place to retire to. As he thought of dreary-skied Moscow in comparison, he wondered if Rominev had had similar thoughts.

Chapter 65

At the front of an incident room in a Jerusalem police station, Inspector Steiner was busily writing on a felt-tip blackboard. He'd listed every piece of information they had concerning the missing canisters. When he'd finished, he stepped back to admire his work.

"Do you think Perrez was a dupe?" Shavbiz asked.

"With the inflammatory literature we found on his farm, I find it hard to believe he's oblivious to all this," Steiner replied.

"Well, whatever he knows, he's not talking."

Steiner read over what he'd put on the board. Everything had to be right for the briefing he was going to give in an hour.

The most alarming thing he'd written was that Stopowitz and Cohen both had pilot's licences.

"Stopowitz and Cohen disappearing at the same time as the canisters arrived in Israel can't be a coincidence," he concluded.

"If they've got the canisters, are they mad enough to use them?" Shavbiz asked.

"The fact that they've smuggled them in, tells me we should assume they are," Steiner said. "You've heard the mad impassioned speeches of the extremists. Do you think they're capable of spraying deadly germs on the Palestinians, Shavbiz?"

Shavbiz had heard the hatred in their voices. He thought they were definitely prepared to use the weapons. "I think they'd be prepared to kill as many Arabs as they think are necessary to cleanse Israel of the Palestinians."

Steiner stared at the blackboard a moment, trying to comprehend what kind of evil could lead a man to this. "I'm sorry to say I agree with you, Shavbiz."

In the corridor, they could hear the sound of the first arrivals. Horror registered on a female police sergeant's face as she read what the *Bacillus Anthracis* bio weapon was capable of doing. The blackboard listed the symptoms from the spores getting into the lungs, followed by coughing, and maybe even the odd moment of feeling better, before the microbes' toxins spread throughout the body, resulting in organ failure.

"Please note that the vaccines to combat the inhalation of the virus only work in the illness's early stages. If we don't find these canisters quickly, we could have a genocidal disaster on our hands," Steiner warned, in an attempt to shock his colleagues into action. "We have to find these canisters."

"Someone out there knows something, and the sooner we find out what, the quicker we get to averting catastrophe."

After the briefing, the officers divided up into search teams. When they were gone, only Shavbiz and Steiner remained.

"I can't see what Stopowitz can achieve by using this weapon," Shavbiz remarked. "With such an indiscriminate weapon, they're likely to wipe out as many Jews as Arabs."

Steiner looked at the weather on his computer. It said that, for the next few days, high pressure would remain in place over the Eastern Mediterranean. "If these psychos are prepared to use these weapons, then they have the perfect weather for it," Steiner declared, shaking his head in dismay.

He could see by the worried expression on Shavbiz's face that he agreed with him. They had to find Stopowitz and Cohen. They *had* to find them, and they had to find them *now*.

Chapter 66

Vassilov looked through his binoculars from the hillside. A man wandered out on the villa's veranda. He was the right height and about the same age as Rominev. The man was wearing sunglasses and a baseball cap, so identification was impossible. Vassilov looked at the photo, decided he needed to get much closer to be certain. This was the fifth villa he'd investigated today.

This was the only villa he'd so far encountered where the occupant was a distinct possibility.

With a sniper's rifle, the veranda would be a clean kill. Working with limited resources in a foreign land, he didn't have the luxury of such weapons. Vassilov hid in a cluster of bushes a hundred meters or so from the property, in order to remain unseen from the veranda. He'd made sure the sun wasn't reflecting off his binoculars. The way the man wandered around the veranda, it was obvious to Vassilov that the villa's occupant was blissfully unaware of Vassilov's presence.

The man wandered back out on the veranda, taking off his sunglasses. Vassilov could see his face now, and it matched the face in the photo he'd found.

An hour later, Rominev left the villa. As Rominev

drove off in his car, a smile descended over Vassilov's usually expressionless face.

Vassilov waited a few minutes until the car's engine was a distant sound. He scurried through the undergrowth until stopping a few yards from the villa's ivy-strewn wall. He waited, assessing both sight and sound. He hadn't seen anybody else at the villa, but he wouldn't take any chances. When he was certain it was clear, he climbed the wall and approached the villa's front door. He looked around him. The villa wasn't wired up with security systems or CCTV, nor did it appear to have any sort of alarm. He paused by the front door a moment before ringing the doorbell. Apart from squawking birds in nearby trees, he was greeted with silence.

He inserted his skeleton key into the lock and unlocked the door. He stepped inside and quickly assessed his surroundings. There were plenty of opportunities inside for an ambush.

Vassilov decided the seclusion Rominev had chosen for his hideout would be his downfall. Vassilov quickly checked over the villa and found it empty. He grabbed a kitchen chair and placed it in the hall near the front door. He made sure the door would obscure where he was seated when opened. Sometimes the direct approach was the best approach.

Vassilov sat down. Now was a time for patience. He had no idea how long Rominev would be. However long he was gone, when he stepped through that front door, Vassilov would be ready.

Chapter 67

Cohen pulled at the handcuffs yet again, a reflex action that never resulted in freedom. Pointless. The handcuffs were just as firmly attached to the radiator as on the hundreds of previous occasions he'd tried to free himself during his captivity. The room was stifling and oppressive. Though the curtains were tightly pulled, allowing some respite from the sun, he could still feel the sun's baking heat through the window.

His prison was a strange mixture of Islamic pamphlets, paper, and ink cartridges. He'd long ago decided the room was the storeroom for an Islamic printing press. He was in the center of the spider's web. Being Jewish, he expected no mercy from his captors. He stretched his hand and was just able to reach the bottle of water left for him. He drank greedily, working on the assumption that his captors could take the bottle away from him at any moment.

The regular food and water they supplied had somewhat alleviated his fears, but still he drank as though it might be his last. Giving him food and water meant that they wanted him alive. It also meant they were probably after a ransom.

He wondered if Stopowitz was still alive. He remembered seeing Stopowitz moments before he had blacked out when they overpowered them at the army checkpoint. That was the last he'd seen of his leader. He decided that his captors would get double the ransom for Stopowitz that they would for him. It meant that Stopowitz must still be alive, too.

In the distance, Cohen could hear the incessant noise of beeping traffic. He was in a city. Precisely, what city, he didn't know. They hadn't gagged him, just given him the stark warning that if he shouted for help, they'd kill him.

All he could hear were Arab voices. Outside, walking past his prison. And Arab voices inside the house he was held in. He sat back against the hard wall, could barely feel any blood flow in his tightly handcuffed hand. He wondered how long he'd been there. It was over a week since his capture. A week of hell. His wife and daughter would be frantically worried after his disappearance.

He thought about how easily they'd both been captured and vowed if he survived this ordeal, he'd never allow himself to be so vulnerable again. This experience would push him on to greater endeavours, ones that would ensure that the Palestinians were finally driven from the West Bank. He reflected on future missions as he glanced at the shabby brown carpet beneath his feet. Buried deep in the shaggy pile he spotted a well-worn and slightly rusted paperclip.

He stretched as far as his foot would reach and almost touched it. He pulled the handcuff chain along the radiator pipe, it allowed him a few more inches. He used his outstretched foot to drag the paperclip toward him. He pressed it between his index and forefingers and examined it.

He'd once seen an escape artist use an uncoiled paperclip to unlock handcuffs and wondered if such a feat was possible for an amateur? Whether it was or wasn't possible, he had nothing to lose by trying. Cohen slowly set to work on the lock with the unfurled paperclip.

Chapter 68

Vassilov's eyes were staring at the front door. He'd been sitting patiently waiting for Rominev's return for three hours. Just when he was thinking about going for a piss, he heard the sound of a car engine approaching the villa. Vassilov steadied the gun in his hand and aimed it at the door.

Outside he heard the driver cut the engine. He heard car doors slam. He could see movement through the frosted glass. The front door swung open. He fired three times. Horror registered on the black girl's face as she fell to the floor, her chest riddled with bullets.

Vassilov tried to level his gun on Rominev, felt a sharp stinging pain in his chest as Rominev shot him first. As Vassilov fell to the floor, his finger pulled the Beretta's trigger, and he fired wildly. Slugs ripped into the wall above the door, causing a plaster snow storm.

Rominev was quickly by the assassin's side, kicking the gun out of his reach. "Who sent you?" he shouted.

The man smiled but refused to reply. Rominev searched him, found his wallet and credit card. He studied them. "Did Chernekov send you?"

The man still remained silent.

"I'll get you a doctor if you answer my questions."

"I'm beyond the need of a doctor, comrade." A pool of blood was starting to envelope the floor around Vassilov's body. He was almost dead and decided nothing mattered now. "Chernekov did put this contract out on you, but Chernekov is dead…"

The man's head tilted to the side as he died.

Rominev checked his pulse to confirm that fact. He checked the prostitute he'd picked up in a bar off Sam Sharpe Square for signs of life. Both were dead. It left big problems. He shut the front door and then searched the villa. When sure that nobody else was there, he went to the bar and poured himself a large brandy.

People had seen him leave the bar with the prostitute. When she didn't return, questions were sure to be asked. Rominev decided he had a matter of hours rather than days to sort out this mess. He'd bury the bodies in the hills after dark. He'd rigorously clean the villa, destroying any evidence of murder. By morning, he'd vacate the villa and leave Jamaica.

He removed everything from the pockets of the dead bodies. He wrapped them in sheets before preparing for departure. The car keys meant he had to find the assassin's car and dispose of it.

The blood on the terracotta floor was sticky, taking a lot of effort to remove. Once the room was clean, he set out on his search. Within an hour, he found the man's car on a nearby slip road.

He drove the car a few miles from his rented villa and parked it in a side street. He left the keys in the ignition and the door open, making it easy to steal. When he arrived back at the villa a couple of hours later, there was still a few hours until dark. Rominev would wait until the cover of night to do his darkest work. He had found over the years that the night hid a multitude of sins.

Chapter 69

Pasha looked at Culani, the crane driver, seated before him in the interview room. Culani's face had taken on an alarmingly pale quality. Knowing you were in a heap of trouble and that the charges weren't going to be dropped could have that effect.

"We know that you're not a terrorist," Pasha said. "If you'd known that there were dangerous biological warfare weapons inside the containers, then I'm sure you'd never have got involved in helping getting them into Egypt."

"Like I said, I don't know what you're talking about," Culani reiterated.

"Don't be a fool," Casarak suggested. "We're going to prove that these weapons were smuggled into Egypt through Alexandria. Once we've got that confirmation from other sources, then any testimony you give in a bid to save yourself will be pointless."

"Sergeant Casarak is right. If you've got any intention of trying to save yourself, then this is the moment." Pasha could see Culani was weakening. "If you're worried about your family, then we can arrange police protection for them."

"Police protection costs money, money the police

don't have. Once I've testified, the police will quickly abandon me," Culani decided.

"If information you give us leads to the recovery of these weapons, I'm sure the government will help set your family up under a new identity."

"What have you got to lose?" Casarak interjected.

"Whoever you unloaded the containers for will now know that you've been taken in to answer police questions. They'll probably conclude that you've talked. If we let you go, they'll decide they have to kill you to silence you."

"It'll be easy to let it be known among police informers that you grassed," Pasha pointed out.

"I haven't told you anything," Culani protested.

"That doesn't matter. Your terrorist friends don't know that," Pasha said, turning to Casarak. "I want it put around to all police informers that Mr. Culani has been very helpful to the police. Tell them that, thanks to his information, we shall shortly be making some arrests."

Culani stared blankly at Pasha, contemplating what such an action would mean to him. "I never should have got involved with them. If it wasn't for Kalhid, I wouldn't have."

"Mr. Kalhid, the manager of the company you worked for is involved in this?" Pasha asked, looking at Casarak.

Culani nodded. "And you guarantee my family's protection if I tell you everything I know?"

"You have my word, the police will protect them," Pasha said.

"Then I'll tell you everything." And Culani did. Soon after he had ratted on his accomplices, the police brought Kalhid in for questioning.

"Mr. Kalhid, we've got a witness who says that you paid him a thousand dollars to unload a container off the

Russian container ship *Vladimar*. The witness says that you had him put it back on board an hour later."

Kalhid laughed. "Do you know how many containers we unload a week, Chief Inspector? Did you ask your witness how many containers he unloads a week?"

"This wasn't just any container, Mr. Kalhid, this was a particular container that you specifically asked him to secretly unload from the *Vladimar* when customs officials weren't around."

"Your witness has a fertile imagination, Chief Inspector. He probably stole the money and then told you the first thing he thought would get him off the hook," Kalhid said, laughing.

"And where would a dock worker get the chance to steal a thousand dollars, Mr. Kalhid?" Casarak interjected.

"I wouldn't know," Kalhid said. "I have nothing to do with my staff once they're outside the dock gates."

"I believe him, Kalhid," Pasha said. "I believe he's telling the truth, and you're involved in this."

"He's lying, I assure you."

"And why would he lie?" Pasha growled.

"He's lying because he's got something to hide. Stop harassing innocent citizens like me and find out what he's hiding."

"I think he's telling the truth, and you're lying, Kalhid," Pasha declared. "Have you any idea what you've done? We suspect that the container you unloaded was carrying biological weapons, weapons sold to Islamic fundamentalists by the Russian mafia. Do you know how many people such a weapon would kill if released in a major city? Well?"

Kalhid looked twitchy. "I'm not saying anything until you get me a lawyer. Surely, holding me like this, because of the lies one of my employees tells, isn't legal?"

"Under Egypt's anti-terrorist laws, if we deem you're a threat to society, we can hold you a lot longer." Pasha chortled. "Sit tight, you might be here a long time."

Kalhid thought of the repercussions. Omah's followers had obviously lied to him. They'd told Kalhid that the container was filled with small arms weapons for use in terrorist actions in Israel against the Jews. The fact that the police were interviewing him told Khalid that Culani had talked.

Kalhid's options were limited. His anger at Omah for duping him meant he was tempted to tell the police everything. Any thoughts of betrayal were quickly tempered by the thoughts of prison that any admission of involvement would bring. In prison, Omah's followers could get to him easily. A prison sentence meant almost certain death.

"I meant what I said about not saying anything until I see a lawyer."

"If I were you, I'd stop looking to a lawyer to save you and start trying to help yourself," Pasha said. "Let's stop for a moment and examine the situation. You've foolishly taken money for cargo smuggling without realizing lethal biological weapons were in the container. I won't lie to you. You'll be facing prison for smuggling, but if you cooperate, I can promise you that your sentence will be drastically reduced."

Kalhid thought about what would happen when Omah's followers found out he had been taken in for questioning. They'd decide he must have talked, and retribution would be swift and final. "How can I snitch on smugglers I know nothing about, Chief Inspector?"

"You disappoint me, Mr. Kalhid," Pasha snapped. "So much so that I'm going to make sure the courts throw the book at you."

So be it, Kalhid thought. He was going to stick to

denying everything. He'd hidden the money Omah had paid him. If the police couldn't find evidence of any wrongdoing, then he had a chance. All they had at the moment was Culani's testimony. With that in mind, Kalhid decided his best defense was silence.

Chapter 70

Karaschelki answered his office phone. The line crackled slightly but nobody spoke and silence greeted him. He was about to put the phone down, when Rominev said, "I bet you never thought you'd hear from me again."

"Rominev!" Karaschelki yelled, incredulously.

"At least you remembered my name, Officer."

"Nobody will ever forget you, Rominev," Karaschelki said, signalling to a colleague outside the office to try to get a trace on the call. The colleague picked up another phone to arrange the trace.

"Let's hope some of the memories are fond, Officer."

"Hardly. You killed police officers and were involved in gangland shit. If you're looking for absolution, you've come to the wrong guy."

"I see your point. I can understand that you're bitter. I know what I did, and I'm not proud of it, but maybe what I'm about to give you will lessen your hatred." Rominev noted that Karaschelki hadn't slammed the phone down on him. Maybe, he was interested, but Rominev wasn't naïve. He knew that Karaschelki was also trying to keep Rominev on the line to trace the call.

"And what are you going to give me?" Karaschelki asked.

"I'm going to give you information that will break the underworld stranglehold the mafia has on Moscow. When I fled, you must've gone through my desk drawers. In the top right-hand drawer there was a key in an envelope."

Karaschelki had spent a lot of time thinking about what the key could be for. "We found it."

"Good, the key is important. That key is to a safety deposit box at the Moscow National Bank. The box is in my name. In that box, you'll find all kinds of evidence against the mafia that I've put together in my time dealing with Chernekov."

"You're a treacherous bastard, Rominev."

"I'm an *alive* treacherous bastard." Rominev hung up. He hadn't given the officer enough time to trace the call. He could picture Karaschelki's angry face as he realized that fact.

Rominev picked up his luggage and walked from the payphone in the passenger lounge over to the British Airways desk. At the reception desk, he checked in with a dazzling strawberry blonde for the flight to New York. He sat on a sofa waiting for the call to board the plane. After the police moved in on all the mafia's Moscow operations, the mafia would have other things to worry about than finding Rominev. He smiled to himself. Or at least that was what he hoped.

Chapter 71

Israeli Prime Minister Rabina sat in his office, reading the report that Security Minister, General Mancin, had handed him. "I want the security forces all put on a state of high alert," Rabina ordered. "What do you think they're going to do with them, Mancin?"

"These people are cranks. They don't react normally. The fact that they're smuggling these terrible weapons into our country shows that they've got something planned, Prime Minister," Mancin warned.

"Make sure every available man's involved in the hunt."

"Every man is, Prime Minister," an irritated Mancin replied.

Mancin decided that Rabina, like most politicians, was showing blatant disregard for how overstretched the army's resources were. As usual, they were asking Mancin to plug holes without manpower or funds.

"If they're mad enough to use these weapons on the Palestinians, the Arab countries in the region will explode, Mancin. As well as the danger to our people from these weapons, we could also be facing an apocalyptic Middle East war," Prime Minister Rabina commented.

"I understand how dangerous the situation is, Prime

Minister, but there's a limit to what the police and army can do. The police have been looking for them for two weeks and still don't have a worthwhile lead. We have Mossad using all their resources to try to find them. If they're hiding in neighboring Arab states, then Mossad will find them, Prime Minister."

"This is not a criticism of you or your men. I realize you're doing the best you can," Rabina replied.

"The extremist settlers that Stopowitz leads claim they know nothing of any of this. They claim that the Palestinians kidnapped or murdered Stopowitz and Cohen. You've read the reports, the farm machine consignment we think the canisters were hidden in was delivered to the farm of a Stopowitz supporter. Soon after the delivery, Stopowitz and Cohen go missing. It can't be coincidence, Prime Minister."

"So the settlers are lying," he asked.

"I think so, Prime Minister." Mancin looked at his watch. "I'd better get back to my men. We'll do everything we can to find them, Prime Minister, you have my word on that."

Mancin left. Rabina sat and contemplated his country's fate. The information Mancin had given him was, for the moment, on a need to know basis. As Rabina prepared for an uncomfortable session before the Knesset putting through proposals for higher taxes, he decided that, for now, that the Knesset didn't need to know. Rabina was the master political illusionist. In the Knesset this afternoon, he intended to show no signs to his colleagues of the possible genocide that awaited them.

Being prime minister wasn't just about being a good politician. To be a good prime minister, you also had to have the ability to act. Today in the Knesset, Rabina was going to show the rest of his party what a good actor he was.

Chapter 72

Cohen could hear Arab voices arguing in the other room. The walls were thin, though not thin enough to hear what they were arguing about. He frantically worked the paperclip in the handcuff's lock, but the lock still wouldn't budge. Sweat poured down his back in the sultry room.

He was about to give up when something in the mechanism began to give. He heard a click and the lock miraculously opened.

Divine intervention, he mused. God wanted him to complete his mission. He slowly flexed his stiff hand. The blood started circulating slowly through his numb fingers as he moved them about. He surveyed the room for a weapon, finding a blunt looking knife in a cabinet drawer.

He edged to the door. It wasn't locked. He opened it slightly and looked through the gap along the corridor. The paint-flecked hallway was empty. He crept out of the room and moved slowly along the corridor. As he passed the room with the Arabs in it, he could still hear their animated conversation.

At the front door, he reached for the handle and was about to open the door, but as he touched the warm metal

the door started to open in front of him. He stepped behind the opening door, but realized he'd never make it
back to his room without being seen. There was no other
option but to act.

A short, stocky Arab entered. Cohen punched him
hard on the side of the head. The Arab's legs folded. As
the Arab fell to the floor, Cohen ran past him out the
door. The sun's penetrating glare almost blinded Cohen
after days in darkness.

He stumbled along the landing, oblivious to glares
from snot-nosed kids and gossiping women, apparently
unaware that the flat he was escaping from was an Islamic prison.

Behind him, he could hear the sound of pounding
footsteps on hard concrete. He stumbled down tight
stairs, crashed down the stairwell, and out in the street.
He elbowed past stern-faced Arabs, glanced back, and
could see men chasing him.

In a side street, he passed illegal traders making a
dodgy deal. He ran through claustrophobic streets surrounded by cramped apartments. A sign said: Qasr-Al-
Aini. He stumbled through crowds. When he looked behind him, his pursuers weren't there.

In the shelter of a shop doorway, he momentarily
rested. He needed time to think, had to get his bearings.
His heart pounded, sweat poured down his back—the
clammy fluid a mixture of tension and exertion. Inactivity
had made his muscles weak and languid.

When certain he'd lost his pursuers, he regained
some composure. He cautiously stepped out in the street,
walked off in the opposite direction of where he'd run
from. The references he found to Cairo in shop signs confirmed that was where he was. He wondered about Stopowitz?

Was Stopowitz being held in one of the other rooms

at the apartment block where Cohen had been held? If Stopowitz had been there, there was nothing an unarmed Cohen could do to rescue him.

He kept in crowds, deciding it was safer that way. In these streets, in the kidnapper's heartland, he was an open target. He had to find a police station or a friendly embassy. He thought about the Egyptian police, corrupt and unreliable. He couldn't be sure of any Arab. How sympathetic would any Arab be toward a Jewish hardliner?

At a cluttered knick-knack shop, he found a map of the city in a basket full of Egyptian maps. He looked at the map. He was two streets from the American embassy. He put the map back in the basket without buying it, received a stern glare from the bushy-bearded shopkeeper.

Cohen was now focussed on finding the embassy. The Americans were Israel's allies, so he was sure he would get help there. He started walking in the direction of the embassy. Judging by the distance from the shop, he was ten minutes from the embassy.

Ten minutes between life and death. He walked faster. In every person he passed in the street he saw a threat. In his captivity, he'd only ever seen one of his kidnappers, so anyone he passed, in theory, could be a member of the kidnap gang. There was imminent danger in these steamy bustling streets. Although death was waiting for Cohen, he wasn't ready to die and had too many reasons to live. He walked on quickly.

Chapter 73

Dravagi slapped Muhmad hard across the face. Muhmad stumbled but managed to retain his footing. He couldn't look Dravagi in the eye, knowing how badly he'd fucked up.

"Imbecile!" Dravagi shouted. "You've endangered the whole operation." He was tempted to pull out his knife and hack the cretin to pieces.

"I went out for food. Narak and Ali were supposed to be watching him," Muhmad protested.

"I left you in charge, Muhmad." Dravagi's comment was met with a frosty silence. "A bad leader always blames his men for his own incompetence."

Narak and Ali averted Dravagi's angry gaze. Both men were relieved that Dravagi was focusing his anger at Muhmad.

"I want everybody out on the streets looking for him. I want all the police stations and embassies covered. He hasn't got any money or a mobile phone. There still might be a chance."

"Dead or alive?" Muhmad asked.

"Alive, if possible. Dead if you've got no choice," Dravagi responded. He was frightened by their ineptitude. These people would soon be running Egypt under

Omah's guidance. Dravagi, due to the buffoons Omah had chosen to run his operation, was starting to see deficiencies in Omah's leadership skills. "What are you waiting for?" he shouted.

Muhmad, Narak, and Ali scurried off to obey his orders. When they were gone, Dravagi rang Omah and explained what had happened, bracing himself for one of Omah's rages. Instead, his disastrous news was met with silence.

Omah quickly came to a decision. "We have to move the plan forward. I want you to prepare to put the plan into action by tomorrow morning at dawn."

"It's too soon, master. We're not ready," Dravagi cautioned.

"We have no choice. Because of your incompetence, there's a danger the Jew might get to the authorities. Our spies within the police say that the Alexandria police are interviewing the crane driver and manager of the shipping firm. The decision is being made for us. We can't risk waiting."

Omah had a point, Dravagi thought, for only God could know what the police could piece together interviewing Culani and Kalhid. "If that's your will, master."

"It is. I want the pilots in place and the canisters fitted to the crop sprayers by the morning," Omah ordered.

"It will be done," Dravagi said, but with serious doubts that bringing the plan so far forward was possible. Upon concluding the conversation, he placed the calls necessary to move the plan forward.

Everybody protested. Dravagi expected nothing else. Changing the plan at such short notice created problems for everyone involved. It was Omah's wish that it would be done as God expected it to be done. With heavy trepidation in their voices, they all agreed to move ahead with the plan.

Dravagi checked on Stopowitz. He was still securely handcuffed to the radiator. Dravagi started packing everything away and moving it all to the corridor by the front door.

They'd have to clear everything out quickly. If they didn't find the Jew and he returned with the authorities, then at least they'd find nothing connecting Dravagi and his men to the operation.

Dravagi posted a lookout, giving them a few minutes' escape time, in the event the police had been alerted. Dravagi swore as he found the paperclip that Cohen had used to pick the handcuff lock. A plan that had been working like clockwork until a few hours ago was now in tatters because of this small clip of metal.

Dravagi decided it was a test from God to see if they were worthy of the faith that God had bestowed on them for this mission. Dravagi thought about the way Omah had reacted. He hadn't panicked, had stayed focused, had shown himself worthy of leading the great cause. With Omah as the leader, Dravagi concluded, they were going to succeed.

If they acted quickly and gave the authorities no reaction time, they could still succeed.

Chapter 74

We found this metal pole—the type the army us-es for roadblocks—buried with some army uniforms close to the road on which Stopowitz and Cohen disappeared," Sergeant Rafhin of the Jerusalem police told Inspector Slemen.

"What did the army say?" Slemen asked.

"The commander for that region believes the road carries a minimum confrontation risk. As it's a low grade security area, the army has never set up a roadblock there," Sergeant Rafhin explained.

"The whole of the West Bank is a danger zone, Sergeant," Slemen stated. "Perhaps, if some of the regional commanders came down from their ivory towers once in a while they'd realize that fact."

"Well, the army knows nothing about it, sir."

"Do you think this adds credence to the settlers' argument that Stopowitz and Cohen have been kidnapped?" Slemen asked.

"I think, after this discovery, we have to look at kidnapping as a possibility, sir."

"Maybe it was planted there by the settlers to make us think that Stopowitz and Cohen were kidnapped," Slemen suggested. "One thing you learn in detective work, Rafhin, is never to take things at face value."

"I still think it's a kidnapping, sir. They buried the stuff well away from the road. If it was planted by the settlers and they wanted us to find it, I'm sure they would've made it much easier to find than this."

Slemen decided Rafhin was starting to become a decent detective. A good detective always doubted and queried everything. "Maybe they're outthinking us, maybe they want us to think like that, Sergeant."

"So what do we do, sir?"

"I want you to work on the assumption that a PLO fringe group has got them. Gather everything you can from Palestinian informers. Somebody will let something slip."

"What about the settlers, sir?"

"Don't worry about the settlers. I'll put men on to watch them. You concentrate on finding out if the Palestinians have kidnapped Stopowitz and Cohen."

Rafhin left to obey Slemen's orders. Slemen hurried to the incident room where he studied the incident board and, in particular, the intelligence they had on links with the settlers and the *Bacillus Anthracis* canisters. He noted the phone calls from the Egyptian police regarding the unloading of containers in Alexandria. It was all deeply mystifying.

There were dangerous biological canisters out there in somebody's hands, and Slemen reluctantly concluded he hadn't a clue what was going on.

Chapter 75

Cohen was finding it hard to concentrate. He hadn't had a drink of water for hours. He was dangerously dehydrated. As a result of the dehydration, the congestion, and oppressive heat of early afternoon Cairo, he was struggling to maintain his focus. He reached a sign pointing down a road for the British Embassy. He remembered from the map that the British Embassy was close to the American Embassy.

He hurried through the dense smog, his lungs choking from the exhaust fumes of the dense bustling traffic. Ahead, he could see a large imposing building with the Stars and Stripes fluttering on a flagpole above it.

He weaved through the crowd with a newfound purpose. Behind a heavily guarded marine checkpoint, he could see the embassy gates. When he was almost upon them, a man darted from the side. A knife jabbed at him. Cohen felt a sharp penetrating pain rip into his side. He strode on, fleeing the knifeman. His body went numb, and blood was seeping through his shirt. Cohen staggered toward the barrier. The black marine sentry eyed him nervously.

"Stop where you are, sir!" the marine shouted, raising his weapon.

"I must see someone," Cohen mumbled, falling forward on hard dusty concrete. Through blurred vision, he could see the sentry talking to someone on his walkie-talkie.

People gathered around Cohen. A man tried to stop Cohen's bleeding by wrapping a headscarf around his wound. Cohen was finding it hard to breathe. It felt like his lungs had been ripped to pieces.

Medics arrived and the paramedics treated him before gently placing him on a stretcher. When they were sure that he was stable, the paramedics loaded him into the back of an ambulance, and he was driven away.

Ali, who'd stabbed Cohen, looked on nervously with increasing apprehension. His knife thrust had been deep and penetrating. Whether it was hard or deep enough into Cohen's lungs to kill him was impossible to know.

Ali rushed to a waiting car and ordered his colleague to follow the ambulance. The car quickly sped after the it. If Cohen was alive, he could talk, and his talking was something they could never allow to happen. Ali turned to the driver, deciding it was time for desperate measures.

"I want you to catch up with the ambulance. The moment you've caught it, run it off the road."

"We could be killed," the driver said nervously, noting they were already doing sixty in a built-up area.

"If we die, then it's the will of Allah," Ali said calmly, putting his own foot over the top of the driver's on the accelerator pedal and pinning it to the floor.

Chapter 76

"Move, Jew," Dravagi ordered, nudging Stopowitz along the corridor at gunpoint.

Stopowitz was walking sluggishly. Dravagi couldn't work out if it was genuine sluggishness because he'd been chained up in the same position for days, or if he was delaying things, trying to look for an opening to escape.

They were soon outside the apartment and moving along the landing. Stopowitz noted the three armed men around him. There was to be no escape here. Dravagi was right behind Stopowitz, watching his every move in the inky dark of the early evening twilight.

"If you let me talk to my people, I can negotiate a higher ransom for me—"

"Just do as you're told and walk!" Dravagi ordered.

They reached the bottom of the stairs where Stopowitz was bundled in the back of a van. Dravagi considered binding the Jew's hands, but couldn't risk rope burns. They were so close to D-Day now that they couldn't afford to leave any evidence of their wrongdoing.

Dravagi and one of his men jumped into the back with Stopowitz, while a third man drove. Dravagi told Stopowitz to lie face down on the floor. Stopowitz obeyed. The van weaved its way through the traffic. Stopowitz wondered where Cohen was now.

The fact his kidnappers hadn't killed Stopowitz was a good sign that Cohen might still be alive, also. If they wanted him dead, surely they'd have killed him by now.

Stopowitz noted the roads became more ragged the longer they drove. At last the van stopped. He could hear the driver talking to someone. A brief conversation and then the van lurched forward for about a hundred meters before crawling to a halt.

Moments later, the door flew open, and they led Stopowitz out the van. They were inside an artificially lit aircraft hangar. They led him to a small office and locked him inside. Stopowitz noted the hectic activity around a crop dusting Cessna in the middle of the hangar.

In the tight confines of the office, he frantically looked around searching for an avenue of escape. The phone was gone. Apart from a desk, chair, sofa, and filing cabinet, everything else from the office had been removed. His kidnappers didn't seem to make mistakes.

There had to be a reason why Cohen wasn't here. Stopowitz sat on the sofa and thought about Cohen. Was the reason Cohen wasn't here because he wasn't needed? Did they only want Stopowitz for the exchange? If they only wanted Stopowitz for the ransom, did that then mean that Cohen was dispensable? If he was dispensable, then there was no need to keep him alive. Stopowitz felt tears forming in his eyes. Was his dear friend, Cohen, dead?

Chapter 77

The ambulance darted speedily through traffic. Ali's car was close on its tail. At high speed, the driver turned frantically through the dense traffic. He narrowly avoided a bus that pulled out in front of him. In spite of the bus driver's furious reaction, Ali's car ignored it and sped on.

"We're going too fast!" Ali's driver shouted.

"Stay with the ambulance," Ali ordered.

They'd come too far to give up now. The ambulance turned into heavy traffic, slowing suddenly while cars pulled over to let it pass. Ali leaned across and grabbed the steering wheel. He aimed the car at the back of the ambulance.

"Don't be a fool!" Ali's driver shouted.

The driver tried to wrestle the steering wheel back into his control. Ali was too strong. He was filled with the strength of Islamic zeal. Their car smashed into the back of the ambulance. The driver's head crashed through the windscreen. Ali, wearing a seatbelt, thumped against the dashboard and blacked out.

Ali awoke moments later, dazed and confused. Through hazy vision, he could see his arm covered in splintered glass. Blood seeped down his face from a gaping head wound. He looked to his side—his driver was dead. The rear of the ambulance had concertinaed on impact. He couldn't see if the ambulance's occupants were dead or alive. In his concussed state, he couldn't make out anything clearly.

He gingerly unclipped his seat belt and pulled on the door handle, but nothing happened. He pulled again but, in his weakened state, he couldn't move it. People gathered around the car. A policeman prevented people from opening Ali's door.

"Stay where you are!" the cop ordered. "Nobody move him until the paramedics arrive."

Above the sound of buzzing in his ears, Ali could hear shrieking sirens. He wondered what reception he'd get when the paramedics realized the car he was in had killed their colleagues. Paramedics soon swarmed around Ali, the medics gently removing him from the wreckage.

"What about the people in the ambulance?" Ali asked a cop.

"Just worry about yourself. Their fate is in God's hands," the cop said.

"Keep as still as you can until we've assessed your injuries," the lead paramedic said.

Ali was in no position to argue. His body was numb—his legs were wobbly. The other paramedic moved around the driver's side. A quick examination and a shake of his head toward his colleague confirmed the obvious—that Ali's driver was dead.

As they placed Ali on a stretcher, he could see the ambulance occupants being cut out the wreckage. His last vision before his ambulance door was shut was of a blood soaked Cohen being placed on a stretcher. As his ambulance sped off and Ali drifted off into semi-consciousness, he wondered whether Cohen was alive or dead.

But Ali knew his actions had gained Omah some desperately needed time.

Chapter 78

I'm a Jew and I've been kidnapped," Cohen mumbled, as the medic wheeled him up the antiseptic-smelling corridor toward the Emergency Department.

"Try not to talk, sir. It will be better if you conserve your energy," a young nurse, walking alongside the gurney, said.

"My friend, Leon Stopowitz, was kidnapped with me—I think they're still holding him somewhere in Cairo," Cohen ranted.

The medical staff didn't appear to be listening. Cohen felt the sharp sting of a painkilling injection in his arm. His eyes couldn't focus as the drugs started numbing his senses. The glaring, white corridor lights made him dizzy. He could feel his senses crumbling. As he arrived at the Emergency Department, he couldn't stay awake any longer and blacked out.

When he woke hours later, it took his eyes a while to adjust to his changed circumstances. A nurse busily flitted around him. She propped up his pillow and adjusted his blankets. A young studious looking doctor performed a series of checks on his reflexes.

"I must talk to the police," Cohen said.

"Just relax—you've just had a major operation—you need to rest," the doctor told him.

"I have to see the police. I was kidnapped with a friend back in Israel. I escaped but my friend is still being held captive somewhere in Cairo by the kidnappers. You have to help him, please."

The doctor and nurse had a discussion at the back of the room. The nurse left the room. Cohen drifted back to sleep.

When he woke again, there was a middle-aged man in a shabby suit standing at the end of his bed.

"I'm Sergeant Hamanhi of the Cairo police. The hospital staff say that you claim you were kidnapped."

"I was kidnapped with a friend outside Jerusalem. My friend is being held somewhere in Cairo," Cohen explained.

"And you are?" Hamanhi asked.

"My name's Cohen, my friend is Leon Stopowitz."

Hamanhi wrote down some notes in a tatty looking notebook.

After a few minutes, the doctor appeared. "The patient needs some rest. You'll have to go, Sergeant."

Hamanhi left the room, knowing better than to argue with irate medical staff. Outside the hospital, he rang his commander and arranged for an armed guard to be stationed outside Cohen's hospital room. They needed to consult the Jews, find out if there was any credence in Cohen's story.

If this Stopowitz had, in fact, been taken, they'd need his photo to distribute among the Cairo police divisions.

Hamanhi would do what he could but it would take time. The fact that Cohen had escaped, and the kidnappers knew that their kidnapping racket was up, meant Stopowitz's life was in grave danger.

If they didn't receive a ransom demand for Stopowitz very soon, then Hamanhi could come to only one conclusion. Stopowitz was dead.

Chapter 79

Steiner grabbed the file from Slemen. He sat back in his high-backed chair and read it. "None of this makes sense. I was convinced Stopowitz and Cohen were involved in a terrorist plot, yet Cohen has been admitted with stab wounds to a Cairo hospital."

"The Palestinians must've kidnapped them and taken them over the border," Slemen said.

"But what about the container the canisters were smuggled in. Why was it sent to Perrez's farm? There's an established connection with the extremist settlers and the canisters, yet the fact that Cohen escaped his kidnappers and is lying in a Cairo hospital contradicts everything we know."

"We'll find the answers in Egypt," Slemen said.

Steiner wondered whether it would be answers or just more questions. Arrests had been made, interrogations were taking place. The frantic search for the canisters was still at the forefront in Israel, but there was still a multitude of unanswered questions remaining.

The settlers, in particular, troubled him. Perhaps, this Egyptian business was a ruse to throw them off the scent.

Steiner was quiet throughout their Cairo flight. He didn't trust the Egyptians. Memories of Yom Kippur stories of the Egyptians' treachery from his war veteran father still resonated in Steiner's head. One thing he'd learnt from talking to his father was that you had to be cautious when dealing with them.

A bright young detective met them at Cairo airport. An hour later, they arrived at a bustling police station in the heart of Cairo.

In an upstairs office, Commander Abulami, a gray-haired baggy-faced official of the Cairo police, was waiting. "I've been told by my government to give you every assistance in your investigation," Abulami stated. "Cohen survived the stabbing and the car crash and has responded well to treatment after the operation."

"We need to talk to him," Slemen said.

"I'm afraid that decision is in the hands of the doctors, Inspector."

"Stopowitz followers could be about to implement a terrorist assault using biological weapons in the region. We need to know what Cohen knows," Steiner pressed.

"I'll pressure them, emphasize the international ramifications," Abulami said. "Let's go through your files and see what you already know."

They exchanged information but, by the end of the exchange, Steiner was even more confused. "So you think the canisters never arrived in Haifa but were unloaded in Alexandria, Commander Abulami?"

"I think so. Culani, under police pressure, talked. He confirmed that the tractor parts container was unloaded for an hour in Alexandria, ample time for the canisters to be removed. This suggests that there are dangerous biological canisters in the hands of Islamic fanatics. I've no doubt that these canisters are somewhere in Egypt," Abulami added.

"My government thinks the canisters were smuggled into Israel by Stopowitz's settlers," Steiner argued.

"That's why we need to speak to Cohen," Slemen pressed. "Only Stopowitz and Cohen know if they were smuggled into Israel or not."

Abulami rang the hospital and, after a brief discussion with the doctor, said. "The doctor says that Cohen is awake but drowsy, but we can speak to him for a few minutes."

When they arrived at Cohen's bedside, he was sleepy but coherent. Abulami stepped back and let the Jew talk, deciding he might learn more by just listening.

"Mr. Cohen, I'm Detective Inspector Steiner of the Israeli police. I've been sent to Cairo to try and find out what's going on."

"They've still got Stopowitz. He's being held prisoner in Cairo," Cohen mumbled.

"You said you were handcuffed to a radiator in an apartment. We need to find this apartment, Cohen. You're going to help us do that," Steiner said.

Abulami produced a map of the city, laying it on Cohen's bed. Cohen eyed it and tried to picture his escape route, but couldn't remember the details. "It all happened so quickly," Cohen said. "I was desperate to flee my kidnappers. I didn't have time to admire the scenery."

"Can you tell us what you remember of the kidnapping?" Slemen asked.

"We were on our way to Jerusalem to see our accountant. We were waved down at an army roadblock, where we were kidnapped at gunpoint. They injected us with something that made us sleep, I woke up on my own in the room, and I haven't seen Stopowitz since. The kidnappers handcuffed my hand to a radiator. I found a rusty paper clip and was able to unlock the handcuff. I was able to escape into the street, and I almost made it to the American Embassy before someone stabbed me."

"Try and remember what you can about this apartment. Even something you think is trivial might help us to find the place," Abulami said.

"There was a lot of traffic noise," Cohen stated. "I could hear people passing by on the landing outside the window of the room I was held in."

What he was describing covered most of Cairo, Abulami thought. He tried another angle. "When you escaped from the apartment, try and picture the street you ran into. Think what was around you, anything that might narrow the search."

Cohen thought about his escape. He'd run down four flights of stairs. He could picture a road and, across the road, he could see a neon-lighted fez above a coffee shop. What he remembered he told Abulami who jotted it down. The doctor soon appeared and told the police Cohen was still weak and, for the moment, the interview was over.

Back at Abulami's office, a sergeant hurriedly spoke to Abulami. "A patrolman knows where a coffee shop that fits Cohen's description is. He says there's an apartment block opposite, sir," the sergeant said.

They all hurried outside to Abulami's car. There was no time to waste. Cohen had escaped the terrorists, but Stopowitz was still missing. The terrorists had caught Cohen at the embassy and brutally stabbed him. Then there was the car ramming the ambulance. The reports from witnesses claimed it was a deliberate act. They were ruthless and brutal, Abulami decided, and regrettably were probably now in possession of deadly biological weapons—weapons, Abulami concluded, they'd have no hesitation in using.

Chapter 80

I want everybody on this floor interviewed," Abulami ordered his underling Sergeant Hamanhi as he stood in the empty apartment they'd decided had been used by the kidnappers.

"Yes, sir," Hamanhi said. He left to carry out Abulami's orders.

"They've cleared this place out." Slemen said.

"Forensics will go over the apartment shortly," Abulami stated.

"This place has been professionally cleared by people who know what they're doing," Steiner remarked.

"None of this makes sense," Slemen said. "If you were going to kidnap Cohen and Stopowitz for ransom, why bother to bring them all the way to Cairo when there are plenty of places to hide them in Israel?"

"You're right. For whatever reason they were brought to Egypt, it doesn't look like the kidnappers were after a ransom," Abulami said.

"I think they were brought to Egypt for a specific purpose," Slemen said.

"There was no need for Cohen and Stopowitz to be brought to Egypt, yet the kidnappers brought them here.

Any idea why the kidnappers would do this, gentlemen?" Abulami asked.

Steiner and Slemen looked dumbfounded. Hamanhi rushed in the room. "A guy on the ground floor of the apartments, opposite the coffee shop, remembers seeing some men acting suspiciously around a van last evening."

"Did he take enough notice to make a note of the licence plate?" Abulami asked.

"He won't say, sir. He says he'll only talk to the man in charge."

"Take me to him," Abulami ordered.

On the ground floor outside the apartment block, a wrinkle-faced old man stood smoking.

"Mr. Mustafa, this is Commander Abulami. He is in charge of the investigation," Hamanhi told Mustafa who suddenly became interested.

"Good, I need to talk to someone who matters," Mustafa said, his hard gray-flecked eyes giving Hamanhi a dismissive look.

"Sergeant Hamanhi says that you have information about a van," Abulami pressed.

"I might have," Mustafa responded, taking a drag from his cigarette.

"What do you mean 'might have'?" Abulami snapped.

"I can see by the number of police that have descended on the apartment block that the van is important to you—"

"What's your point?" Abulami snapped.

"If the people you're after are so important, then there must be a reward for information leading to their capture."

"Just give me the number plate, or I'll have you arrested for obstructing the police," Abulami threatened.

"If you arrest me, then you still won't have the number-plate," Mustafa declared.

Abulami sighed. Out of his wallet, he removed twenty dollars. He waved it in front of Mustafa. "This is yours if you give me the number-plate of the van."

"I was hoping for more," Mustafa said greedily.

"And I was hoping not to have to arrest you because I don't want to fill out the paperwork. It appears, with your obstructive attitude, that you're leaving me no choice, Mr. Mustafa," Abulami said angrily, reaching for his handcuffs.

Mustafa's spindly fingers grabbed the money. Out of his pocket, he took out a slip of paper. Abulami looked at the paper. On it was written the make and plate number of the van. Abulami then dismissed Mustafa.

When he was out of earshot, Abulami said, "Get an APB out on the van, also put out the van details over the TV and radio and offer a reward for information."

"They'll have ditched the van by now," Slemen said.

"I agree, but for the moment it's all we've got."

"I need to ring my people back in Jerusalem," Slemen said.

He walked out of earshot to make the call. It was a conversation filled with dread. Cohen and Stopowitz had been kidnapped and taken to Egypt. The canisters appeared to have been unloaded in Alexandria rather than Haifa. The whole situation was a mess, Slemen decided, as he stood relaying his grim news back to Israel over his mobile phone.

Chapter 81

The first tentative orange-purple flecks of dawn broke in the east as Mohammad switched off the light in his tiny security hut next to the airfield. He was listening to the radio and looking at the latest porn mag his brother, who lived in Holland, had sent to him.

Mohammad was amazed at the lengths of degradation Western girls would go to in these magazines. As he could feel an erection coming on, he was truly grateful for their depravity. As he studied a blonde on page seven doing unspeakable things with a cucumber, the hourly news came on the radio. The newscaster announced a government job creation initiative, before switching to a story about kidnappers and a reward for information on the whereabouts of a white van. After a brief description of the van, the newscaster went on to stress the importance of finding it, before finally giving the licence plate number.

Mohammad thought back to yesterday. A white van had entered the airfield carrying laundry. It hadn't been the usual driver and had taken an hour longer than usual to drop off the laundry to the reception buildings. He remembered the number plate of the van also had a five in it. Rather a coincidence, he thought.

He hesitated with his hand over the phone, wondering if he was being an idiot. He thought about what he could do with the reward money. For a start, he could visit his brother in Amsterdam. A trip like this would normally be way beyond his means. Any reward money would suddenly make the trip more feasible.

He studied the nude picture in the magazine of the girl fingering herself and decided he might use the money to fund a camera study course. Whatever he did with the money, he wouldn't get it unless he took the risk. So what if he made himself look stupid by ringing the police?

He called them and, to his surprise, they were very interested, saying they'd send someone immediately. The message was relayed to Abulami. He checked out the laundry firm who delivered to the airfield, and they had no record of dropping off laundry at the airfield yesterday.

"We might be in business," Abulami stated as they all jumped in his car and got moving.

As they drove, Slemen was the first to speak. "The *Bacillus Anthracis* canisters are meant to be sprayed from an in-flight aeroplane. If the van does, in fact, belong to the kidnappers' and they're at an airfield, then there's a danger they might be about to use the weapon."

"We don't know that," Abulami cautioned. "Anything on our part at the moment is just supposition and conjecture."

Whatever it was, Slemen noted that Abulami speeded his car up. Slemen found this action encouraging. It also demonstrated that Abulami was listening to what Slemen said and that the Egyptians were taking this dangerous threat to the region's security seriously.

Chapter 82

Stopowitz studied the dimensions of the office for what seemed like the thousandth time since he'd been first brought in. In the hangar outside, he could hear hectic activity and maintenance work being carried out on a crop spraying Cessna. He'd noticed the plane just before he was bundled into the office.

He thought about Cohen. Was Cohen dead or alive? Stopowitz hadn't seen his friend since their kidnapping back in Israel. He wondered if his wife and kids had given up on him. As he reflected on recent events, the banging in the hangar suddenly stopped. He moved to the door, attempting to listen to their conversation. He could hear snippets but nothing clear enough to make out what they were talking about.

There were no weapons in the room, nor were there sharp edges or broom handles to use as a club. Apart from a sofa with a couple of cushions on it and a small empty filing cabinet, there was nothing to aid an escape attempt. Cunning and guile would be his only weapons. He gathered the cushions together on the sofa, and tried to shape them into the figure of a man.

They were too small. He took out a filing cabinet drawer. He laid the drawer on the sofa between the cushions. He fashioned a cushion as a head and then laid his jacket over the filing cabinet. It looked like a body apart from the legs. He took off his trousers, ripped open the other cushion and stuffed the trouser legs with padding.

He stood back and admired his work. He concluded it wouldn't fool anybody for more than a brief glance. When they opened the door to see if all was well, he thought he might have a moment to act. But was it enough? If they thought he was lying on the sofa, it might just give him a chance.

There was no time to consider. Outside he could hear the sound of approaching voices. Stopowitz stood behind the door. He'd only get one chance. At the door, he heard the sound of a key being inserted in the lock. The key slowly turned. The sound of the turning key seemed to be amplified by his nervous senses. There was only one price that could be paid for failure now, and that price would be death.

As the door began to open and Stopwitz prepared himself for the assault, he could sense the angel of death hovering over him.

Chapter 83

All the final safety checks had been made on the Cessna and the plane was ready for take-off. Dravagi motioned to the plane's mechanic as he took one last look in the cockpit. "We can't afford any mistakes," he said.

"The plane is ready," the mechanic assured him. "There won't be any mechanical failures, you have my word on this."

Dravagi walked to the hangar door and looked out at the distant purple-orange dawn. He wanted the Cessna to be in the air by seven o'clock. By eight o'clock, he wanted the Cessna over the dispersal zone, preparing to release its deadly load on the unsuspecting masses.

He checked the ampoules and syringe in his bag and then ambled across the hangar to the office where Stopowitz was being held. He listened a moment by the door. The office was quiet. From his pocket, he removed his Browning pistol, inserted the key gently in the door, and slowly opened it.

Ahead of him in the dark room, he could see Stopowitz lying on the sofa.

He smiled, deciding this was going to be easier than he thought. The door smashed into his side, causing him to fall over. The jolt knocked the Browning out of his grasp. It clattered across the floor, and, as he scrambled for the gun, he saw the trouser-less figure of Stopowitz run out the door.

Dravagi retrieved his weapon and gave chase. As he stepped out the office into the hangar, there was no sign of Stopowitz. There were so many places to hide among the equipment, Dravagi immediately became tense and alert.

"The Jew's escaped! He's somewhere in the hangar!" Dravagi shouted.

His men all stopped what they were doing and began to search.

Dravagi looked at the shut hangar doors, there was no way Stopowitz could've opened and shut the doors without being noticed. Dravagi concluded that Stopowitz must still be in the hangar. "There's no way out, Jew, come out with your hands up and no harm will come to you."

Stopowitz was hidden behind an oil drum. Dravagi was edging toward him from the left, another guy was working around from the right. If he stayed where he was, in a moment it would all be over. He had no choice. Stopowitz leapt up and sprinted toward the hangar doors. Dravagi fired his pistol at the concrete in front of Stopowitz. "Halt!"

Stopowitz was yards from the hangar door. Dravagi was under strict orders not to harm him. As Stopowitz's hand grabbed the hangar door handle, Dravagi decided he had no choice. He fired once into Stopowitz's leg,

Stopowitz's leg buckled beneath him. He stumbled forward and banged his arm on the door as he collapsed to the floor. Stopowitz tried crawling out the door but Dravagi's men quickly descended on him and pulled him back inside. Dravagi pushed them aside, hastily studied

Stopowitz's wounded leg. The wound was leaking blood badly. Dravagi thought of the rollicking he was going to get from Omah for harming the captive. He'd had no choice. He couldn't let the Jew escape.

Dravagi got his men to drag Stopowitz back to the office where he was quickly injected with the tranquilliser to keep him passive during the flight. Dravagi wondered what damage he'd done to their efforts at subterfuge by shooting Stopowitz. When there was an investigation after the attack, it would be noted that Stopowitz had a gunshot wound.

Dravagi had no time to worry about it now. This morning, Omah's plan had to be put in motion. Dravagi ordered his men to put Stopowitz in the cockpit of the plane. If the plan was going to be successful, the Cessna needed to be in the air soon. Dravagi looked at his watch. It was almost seven o'clock. The plane needed to be in the air now.

Chapter 84

id you hear that?" Abulami asked Hamanhi.

"It sounded like a gunshot, sir," Hamanhi said.

Abulami pointed. "It came from that hangar."

He ordered the armed unit deploying from the van to head toward the hangar.

A disgruntled airfield official, who'd appeared from an office, was quickly ushered behind Abulami's car where Abulami awaited.

"Who owns the hangar?" Abulami asked.

"It's owned by an agricultural company who sprays fields for the farmer's crops," the official responded. He studied the frenzied police activity with nervous interest and had already decided this was serious and he'd fully cooperate.

"Is there anybody from the company there at the moment?" Abulami pressed.

"I really couldn't tell you. They come and go as they please, Officer. If they pay their bills on time and don't cause any trouble, we don't keep much of a check on them."

"Well, they're about to cause you a *lot* of trouble," Abulami warned.

His attention was now drawn to the SWAT team creeping around the hangar's side. Just as they approached the hangar door, it flew open and Abulami could hear the roar of a Cessna's engine.

A gun battle erupted around the entrance to the hanger. Dravagi ran out, firing wildly with his Browning. Two of the SWAT team were shot at point blank range and fell dead on the grass.

The Cessna shot forward out on the runway. The pilot pushed the plane to full throttle and roared along the dry brown grass. Dravagi engaged the SWAT team in a brief gun battle. When his ammunition ran out, the SWAT team's bullets ripped his body to pieces.

As Dravagi lay dying, Abulami and Hamanhi jumped in Abulami's car and sped after the plane. The Cessna was gathering speed. Abulami pumped his accelerator, rammed the back of the plane just before it was able to take off.

The plane pin-balled off the runway, crashing into a fence. Abulami fired several rounds at the cockpit. The glass splintered, and blood and flesh splattered all over the cockpit. The pilot lay across his instruments, dying. Around the hangar, the gunfight ended as the last of Dravagi's men died.

Abulami wasn't interested in the gun battle. His eyes were now fixed on the plane that must be carrying the deadly canisters. As he got close to the cockpit, he couldn't hear anything above the thrumming of the Cessna's engine. In the cockpit, he could see the pilot's hand move toward the instrument panel and press a button.

A huge gush of spray whooshed out of the plane's crop spray tanks. The spray hit Abulami square in the face. He desperately covered his mouth and nose with his jacket. He coughed and spluttered, knowing he'd inhaled the deadly bacteria and was now a dead man walking.

He staggered forward and reached the cockpit. He clambered in the cockpit and fired several rounds at the

Arab pilot. The pilot died with barely a whimper. Abulami leaned across the pilot and clicked off the switch that said *SPRAY*. Abulami staggered from the plane, Hamanhi and Slemen rushed toward him.

"Get back! He's sprayed the canisters!" Abulami shouted.

"Clear the airfield!" Hamanhi shouted to the others as Hamanhi and Slemen quickly retreated. Cops pulled their shirts over their faces in a feeble attempt to avoid inhalation as they fled the scene.

The airfield was cleared in a matter of minutes. Abulami stood motionless, his eyes fixed upon the wreckage. He noted the lack of wind meant the spray wasn't being dispersed but just lingered around the plane. Suddenly a hand grabbed Abulami and led him away. Abulami looked to his side. Hamanhi, with his face covered, pushed Abulami in the back of a waiting squad car. Hamanhi got in the driver's seat and with the squad car's siren wailing spirited Abulami away. As they sped toward the hospital, more police units passed them trying to cordon off the airfield.

"I've radioed a security message to all Egyptian airfields, warning that a biological attack using crop spraying planes is imminent, sir," Hamanhi stated as he drove.

Abulami had so many questions running around in his head. He was angry with Hamanhi for risking his life trying to save him. "You should have left me, Sergeant. You openly disobeyed an order and put your life at risk," he yelled, his voice trembling with fear.

"Would you have left me, sir?" Hamanhi asked with a faint smile.

Abulami knew he'd never leave one of his men. "That's not the point," he responded weakly.

"It's exactly the point, sir, save your energy."

And with that, Abulami drifted off to a choking sleep

as the deadly virus began to take hold of his respiratory
system.

Chapter 85

Mullah Omah sat on his prayer mat in his tent, contemplating the likelihood of the attack's success. He glanced at the satellite TV, eagerly waiting for the panic-stricken news bulletins that were sure to appear when the government buffoons realized their empire was crumbling around them and the new Egypt was about to begin.

He thought of the people rising up against their government oppressors. In Egypt, there'd been a succession of unholy governments who'd made many treacherous pacts with the Jews. Omah smiled to himself. These same Jews, who had now proved their treachery by attacking Egypt with biological weapons, were going to be vilified from Cairo to Damascus. The Egyptian government was going to be seen as traitors for colluding with Israel.

Omah praised God as he thought of the bloodletting that was sure to follow when the news of the Jewish attack was made public. God knew that any meaningful change couldn't come about through democratic means. Omah switched channels, frantically trying to find a news bulletin that announced the attack. He tried to see the clock in the corner but his aging eyes meant the clock face was just a haze. He reluctantly put on his glasses and could then see that the attack had started three hours ago. Three hours was plenty of time for news of the attack to have reached the local and international news channels.

He wandered outside where some of his followers sat drinking coffee and listening to a radio. "Has Dravagi sent news?" Omah asked.

"Sorry, master, we've heard nothing from Cairo," a young follower reluctantly told him.

Omah rounded on him. "I must know what's happening!"

"They'll phone us when there's news, master," another follower said.

Omah sighed. "By now we should've heard something."

He was pulled from his thoughts by a strange humming noise that could be heard over the horizon. He was starting to have serious doubts about having based his command center openly out in the desert. But there wasn't much of a choice in the matter. The command center had to be well away from the cities to alleviate any risk of spore inhalation after the attack.

On the radio, there was a sudden news bulletin. The announcer confirmed that there'd been an attempted terrorist attack on Cairo and other Egyptian cities. A cheer rang out around the camp, but it was quickly followed by despair when the announcer said the attacks had been thwarted, and that planes carrying biological weapons had been stopped from taking off by anti-terrorist units.

Omah's face reddened with anger. His followers had not proved worthy enough in God's eyes. It was as he held this thought that the Apache Links helicopter swooped over the top of the hill with its cannons spitting death on the campsite. The sand was swamped in a wind cloud of sand and dust. Omah's followers desperately ran for cover, dying as they fled.

They'd been compromised by one of the men they'd sent out on the mission, Omah concluded, as small arms fire erupted from the campsite, and his men fired at the helicopter. Omah tried to run but his aging legs weren't used to such violent physical activity. He fell as a hail of bullets whizzed and pinged across the campsite. As he lay in the dust, Omah's frail legs were torn to pieces by flesh-ripping bullets. He lay dying, along with his followers, as the Apache helicopter sped off to the east.

When the cannon's death rattle ceased and silence began to settle over the camp, the groaning of the dying and wounded could be heard. As the Apache turned around for another sweep, Omah looked at his broken body and knew it was God's chosen moment for him to die. In his death throes, Omah had one last act of contrition. Just as the Apache swooped back in on the campsite, Omah turned his broken body in the direction of Mecca and prayed for deliverance.

Chapter 86

Stopowitz and his followers stood by the gate as the ambulance trundled past the Palestinian protesters. There didn't seem to be as many protesters as before his kidnapping. He didn't know why. Maybe it was the media and the reports of Mullah Omah's evil plan that had made them less virulent. Stopowitz didn't care what the reason was. All he cared about was the fact that there weren't as many, and this would cause less of a hindrance to his sect's West Bank expansion plans.

The ambulance parked in the compound and Cohen was lowered from it in a wheelchair. Stopowitz waited until Cohen's family had all hugged him, and then Stopowitz greeted his friend. "You saved me, my friend. If you hadn't escaped, they might have succeeded."

"I did nothing. It was God's will that we both survived the kidnapping, God's will that we still need to complete our sacred task," Cohen responded.

Stopowitz looked around him at his followers hanging on Cohen's every word. Only true believers of the cause could give that look. At that moment, Stopowitz had no doubts that they were going to succeed. He and Cohen had survived. They'd survived the worst that the Islamic extremists could throw at them and lived to carry on with their sacred task. The assault by the SWAT team on the hangar meant that Omah's followers hadn't had time to put Stopowitz in the Cessna with the pilot. The office Stopowitz had been locked in had been sealed off from the worst excess of the *Bacillus Anthracis* spray, and a drugged Stopowitz had been rushed to hospital where he'd been treated in time.

Using his cane as an aid, Stopowitz followed the paramedics and Cohen into Cohen's house. Only close family and Stopowitz stood by Cohen's bedside. Cohen had a long road to recovery after his stabbing—weeks of rest and recuperation.

Cohen's wife and children left Stopowitz alone with him while they went and attended to some tasks.

Stopowitz sat by Cohen's bedside. "They almost succeeded, my friend," he commented. "If their plot had succeeded and the world had thought we committed that atrocity—"

"I know, I keep thinking about it. I keep thinking that all our work here would've come to nothing."

"Don't think about it anymore. They failed. They failed, and we have the chance of finishing our work." Stopowitz replied with a smile. "In fact, all they've done by all this is to demonstrate the righteousness of our cause. God was there for us when we needed Him, their God wasn't. The world can see that we were fated by God to complete our sacred task. Soon the Holy Land will be unified under the Jewish faith."

"I shall rest easier knowing that fact," Cohen said.

Stopowitz could see Cohen was starting to doze after his long journey. As Cohen drifted off to sleep, Stopowitz stepped out the room. His friend had earned his rest. Cohen had insured by his actions that both of them lived and could, therefore, complete their mission.

Stopowitz went back to his office, looked at the

planning map of the illegal settlements that they wanted to build, and decided that, on Monday morning, the building of the foundations of the new settlement to the west would start, and the new Israel that Stopowitz would create for his children would be a step closer.

Chapter 87

The Cambridge restaurant was quieter, now that the lunch-time crowd had come and gone. Sarah Appleton had told her father that she didn't want to meet him.

Appleton had pressed, told her he'd be sitting outside the restaurant at a roadside table between midday and two o'clock if his daughter felt like talking.

Appleton sat there, frustrated. Why would Sarah want to meet him? He'd messed up her life, almost gotten her killed. His actions had indirectly led to the murder of Sarah's boyfriend. Appleton drank the last dregs of his coffee, glanced at his watch. It read 2.05—she wasn't coming. He stood up to leave. As he was putting his jacket back on, a hand lightly tapped him on the shoulder. He looked around. Sarah stood behind him. He hugged her. She still had that warm body heat she'd had as a child. They both sat down and stared at each other.

"I didn't think you were coming," he said.

"I nearly didn't. I thought about what you did to me and James. Your actions led to James's murder."

There was an uncomfortable silence between them. A waiter appeared and Appleton matter-of-factly ordered coffee.

Sarah seemed to be looking everywhere except at him. At last, she turned to him and held his stare.

"I never meant for any of this to happen," he pleaded.

"You never mean for anything to happen, but it still does. If you hadn't been involved with underworld figures like Winterburn, the situation would never have arisen. Sometimes, I think you're like the four horsemen of the apocalypse, Dad. Everywhere you go, trouble is never far behind you."

"I got into a situation I couldn't get out of—everything spiralled out of control so quickly." Appleton stared hopefully into Sarah's eyes. "I never meant any harm to you. If I could've saved your boyfriend, I would've. Why did you ring him, Sarah? Why couldn't you have waited until the heat died down before you called him?"

"I loved him. I didn't think I could live without him—" Sarah said in an irritated voice. "—and don't try and blame me for James's death."

"I'd be the last person to blame you after what I put you through. I put you in an impossible position, Sarah, I deserve your hatred."

"I don't hate you, Dad."

"After what I did, you should. I put your life at risk. Now you have to live under a changed identity at uni. I've messed your life up badly, Sarah."

Sarah didn't argue. He had. Until he'd stolen the mob money, Sarah's life had been going swimmingly. Now she went to a psychiatrist regularly, James was dead, and she had to live under an alias. "I want my life to be normal again, Dad."

"It will be, love. I've still got money hidden away in secret Cayman Island accounts—"

"Why do you think every problem in life can be

solved with money, Dad?" Sarah snapped. "James never had money and he was always happy."

Tears began to run down Sarah's face. Appleton tried to move toward her to comfort her, but she waved him away. An uncomfortable silence enveloped the table. Appleton had only just gotten out of prison. They'd sentenced him to three years for his part in Winterburn's world. He'd have gotten double the sentence but for the word the prosecution had put in for him concerning his cooperation with the police.

Sarah was much more womanly than he remembered. Her experiences in France had led to a new hard edge to her character. Appleton had no idea where he stood with his daughter. He barely knew her now. She blamed him for everything and he couldn't fault her. He was looking for a spark, anything that could reignite any kind of relationship between them.

She stood then touched his hand. "This is going to take time, Dad." With that, Sarah left.

Appleton wouldn't run after her. The more he pushed, the harder this was going to be. Sarah needed time to find out what her relationship with her father was going to be.

Appleton would give her time. What else could he do but wait and hope she'd want to have something to do with him?

He watched the back of her until she was out of sight around a corner. Was that the last time he was ever going to see his daughter in his life? If it was, he deserved his fate. With that in his mind, he paid the waiter for his bill and left.

Chapter 88

The smart-suited man in the lounge gave Rominev a glance and a stare. The stare was held for a brief few moments, then the man headed for the lift and was gone. Rominev finished his beer at the bar. It was nothing. These things were always nothing. Since his arrival in New York three years ago, his twitchiness with strangers was abating, as he realized that events in the Russian underworld had moved on, and he was now off the radar.

Rominev rented an apartment on the third floor of the building across the street. He was a regular frequenter of the hotel bar, to such an extent that he was on first name terms with the barmen, he was in there that often. It was as he put his empty glass down on the bar that he noticed her in the corner. Gorgeous legs, beautiful eyes, the center of attention in any bar.

She drifted up to the bar and ordered a gin and tonic. She had smooth red nails and lips, stunning porcelain-colored skin—skin that said, I don't work for a living. She sat on a leather bar stool and stared into her drink with a world-weary glare.

Rominev was assertive. A lonely soul in a foreign land couldn't afford to be anything else. "Are you staying at the hotel?" he asked in his now perfect English. Three years in New York encountering Americans daily, coupled with study on his laptop, had led to fluency.

"Are you talking to me?" the woman asked, running her eyes over him.

"Well, I wasn't talking to the bar stool," he said.

"I don't usually talk to strangers in bars," she said then sipped her drink nonchalantly.

"My name's, Gregor, now I'm no longer a stranger," he said.

She hesitated a moment. "I'm Carol, from Wisconsin," she finally ventured.

"Well, Carol, from Wisconsin, what brings you to the Big Apple?"

"For starters, I didn't come here to be chatted up by lounge lizards in bars."

Rominev laughed. "I suppose you didn't."

"I'm here visiting my sister. I'm staying at the hotel because she hasn't got room for me with her kids at the apartment."

Rominev slowly unlocked her with his charm—the art of chatting up women was to make them feel at ease, make them think that they were special. You had to at least put on the pretence of being a good listener. He had learned the ways of the Americans well in his three-year tenure in the city.

When it was close to midnight, he made his move. A nightcap in her room. She hesitated—most of them did—deciding if he was a threat or not. Rominev's first name terms with the barmen always eased any worries, and Rominev wasn't surprised when she invited him to her room.

They necked like teenagers during the lift journey. Rominev was already undoing some of her blouse buttons when she fumbled the key into the lock of her room. As they crashed onto the sofa, removing clothes, Rominev suddenly became aware of a presence. He leapt to his feet. In the flickering light from a neon advertising sign across the street, he saw him. It was the man he'd stared at in the lounge earlier. He saw the silenced Beretta in the man's hand, and it was at that moment that Rominev knew.

"Traitors are never forgotten, Comrade," the man said, then fired three times into Rominev's chest at point-blank range.

Rominev fell to the floor. As he lay there, contemplating his folly, he decided that getting too well known in the hotel bar had been his big mistake. There were Russian expats. Word got around. Under the influence of booze over the years, whatever he'd said that had given the game away he'd never know.

As he lay dying, he looked at the blonde who was obviously in cahoots with his assassin. A femme fatale, the ultimate bait, she'd certainly hooked him, Rominev thought.

Chapter 89

The street was quiet now. Too quiet. Hamanhi looked at the body lying burned and charred in the street before him, and he couldn't help but wonder how desperate a man would have to be to do this.

It had been three years since Abulami's death in the hospital from the deadly spore inhalation. Three years since the army had taken control, in the aftermath of Omah's failed attack.

Hamanhi was now in charge of his section, in charge of battling Islamic extremists in Cairo. He wandered over to the body. The forensics guy lifted the blanket so he could take a look. He looked. The face was barely recognizable. It was a man, the singed beard confirmed it. Hamanhi was glad it was a man. If women started performing such abominations in the street, then what would become of their society?

Detective Sadat walked up to Hamanhi. "I've spoken to witnesses, sir. They say that the guy stood in the middle of the street, gave a lecture on Islamic fundamentalism and the illegality, in the eyes of God, of the government. It was as he finished speaking and some uniforms headed toward him to arrest him that he poured petrol over his body and set fire on himself."

"Barbaric," Hamanhi declared.

"I'd say it was more desperation, sir." Sadat was then summoned over to a uniform who'd found another witness.

Hamanhi was starting to feel out of touch with the younger generation. He regarded the torched suicide as total lunacy, whereas Sadat looked at it as a desperate act. Sadat came from a poor family background, had lived among the Cairo slums right in the breeding ground for such random acts of terror. Sadat was closer to these people than Hamanhi would ever be—close enough to understand them.

Hamanhi walked slowly back to his car. Since the army crack-down in the wake of the Omah plot, all the Islamic hard-liners had either fled the country or gone underground. He called in more units to seal the area off. The fewer people who witnessed such actions, the better, he had decided long ago.

Abulami had died to prevent the country falling into the hands of the extremists. As Hamanhi stepped into his car to go back to his office, he wondered what his colleague had died for. The situation in Egypt was getting worse.

The poverty and squalor of the big cities were too much of a breeding ground for the fundamentalists. Until poverty was wiped out in his homeland, the extremists were always going to be there, offering their quick fix solutions.

As Hamanhi drove away, he noted the hateful glares of the gathered crowd around the police cordon. He was regarded as the enemy by most who watched him go. The lunatic who'd torched himself in the road would be hero-worshipped as a martyr.

Egypt was a country engulfed in madness, Hamanhi decided. He also concluded that the militant Islamic threat was always going to be there, and Abulami had died for nothing.

The End

About the Author

Paul Howard was born in the Garden of England, in East Kent, and educated at Castlemount Secondary school, a school that closed thirty years ago. He's always felt lucky to be surrounded by such a wonderful coastline and has fond memories of days spent on the beach as a kid. His deceased father, Mike, was a seaman, who often used to regale him with tales from his overseas trips, including catching strange fish in New Zealand and of his friend, Vic, who used to bare-knuckle fight at fairgrounds in Australia.

Howard lives with his partner, Anna-Maria, a German woman, whose great uncle was Max Brauer, a former prime minister of Hamburg. In the 1930s, Brauer was involved in trying to stop Hitler from coming to power. The resultant success of the Nazis meant that he had to flee Germany for Manhattan before he was arrested. Howard's partner's family has an interesting past, with her deceased English father, a special forces commando in World War Two, receiving commendation letters from Winston Churchill for his bravery in the conflict.

In the 1980s, Howard worked for Hoverspeed at Dover International Hoverport. At the time, he never appreciated what a unique job it was. Because of the huge fuel costs, hovercrafts are far too expensive to run these days. The possibility of having passenger-carrying hovercrafts again is something the world will never see. Since 1989 until recently, Howard worked for Royal Mail as a postman, but his partner's disabilities, Ehlers-Danlos Syndrome and other associated conditions, meant he has had to give up work to become a home care-giver.

In his years of working for Royal Mail, he found a sense of community and a level of camaraderie among postmen that you wouldn't find anywhere other than the armed services. Unfortunately, due to his circumstances, it was time to move on, so, alas, he had to leave many friends behind, look to the future, and focus on his writing.

Disciples of Death is Howard's first novel, an international terrorist thriller, set against the turmoil of the Middle East. Previously, Howard has self-published a book of poetry, *Invicta Tales*, and a selection of comedy sketches, *Bish, Bash, Comedy Dash*, on Smashwords. In April, 2015, a short play of his, *The Clearing*, was staged at the Waterloo East Theatre, and produced by Whoop 'n' Wail as part of their May Day production. In a UK lyrics-only song-writing competition, Howard's song, "1982," is currently at the semi-final stage. He's now working on his second novel, *Soul Mate*, a thriller set in Britain, about the hunt for a serial killer.